MOST WANTED

Street stories from the Caribbean

KV-016-082

MOST WANTED

Street stories from the Caribbean

Christborne Shillingford

PAPILLOTE PRESS
London and Roseau, Dominica

First published in Great Britain in 2007
By Papillote Press
23 Rozel Road
London SW4 0EY

www.papillotepress.co.uk

These stories were first published in The Independent, Roseau, and The Tropical Star, Roseau, between 1996 and 2002

A CIP catalogue reference for this book is available from the British Library

ISBN: 0-9532224-3-8
       978-0-9532224-3-8

Cover photograph: Mary Walters (moving figure);
Eva Kingdon (exterior of The Ruins spice shop, Roseau)
Cover design: Andy Dark
Typeset in New Baskerville

Printed in India

ACKNOWLEDGEMENTS

Special thanks to Alwin Bully and UNESCO for initial support. Also to Computer Design and Print Services for typing and draft work.

And to my editor and publisher: it was interesting working with you.

And, of course, thanks to "you" for purchasing this book; enjoy the stories. From author with respect!

Contents

THE BIG SPLASH

It was a rainy afternoon. As a matter of fact it had been raining all day in Roseau Central and I was walking with my little friend, under an umbrella, playing lovey dovey. She was just coming from work and I was doing the honours by escorting her home. And by pure coincidence we were standing next to a big puddle on the road when I heard this knight rider car with its bombastic sound approaching under high speed.

I tried my best, desperately indicating to the invisible driver the puddle of water. Cheups. The man just pass and SPLASH! Just wet us down, oui. And the thing is I was well dressed, modelling Nike, Adidas and so on, the latest style and brand name.

When he realised what he had done, the driver stopped a distance away, reversed, wound down his "darkers" window, and there telling me "he sorry, he sorry". I was so mad and pissed off, I told him angrily, "Sorry, you sorry eh?" It just so happened that a little girl child was passing, carrying a bucket of water. I grabbed it violently from her, and dashed the MF in his dark-glass, sound-system car (I saw smoke coming out of his stereo amplifier).

My satisfaction was short-lived because I then saw him searching frantically under his seat for something. I had a mind it was an offensive weapon. Therefore I stepped back a couple of paces. The guy opened his car door and brandished one long cutlass sharpened back and front!

You know it? I abandoned my little friend and made a run

for it. No! I wasn't ashamed because I always knew that I would prefer to get shot than a big long cut. (That is why whenever I am walking and I see a guy with a cutlass in his hand, especially if he looking mad, I would put a clear distance between us.)

So I tried to outrun the guy and hoped that he would soon give up the chase. You doh hearing! The man behind me like a magnet. I ran up the road towards the police headquarters. Knowing fully well that I wasn't Olympic material, I was hoping to take refuge there. But when I rounded a vital corner, I stepped on an "ital" skin and slick! Beep I was on the asphalt paying some road tax. In less than a second I was back on my feet again. But the worst thing is nobody was trying to restrain the man. What they wanted to see is a hand or neck fly out.

But that fall stopped me from reaching the police barracks so I diverted into Windsor Park and my would-be executioner followed me relentlessly. All how I glanced back, he was there in hot pursuit. He kept repeating: "If I hold you too!.." but not saying what he would do.

I ran through the northern gate, on the riverside, and crossed the Roseau river barely touching water – I guess you know how difficult it is to run on dry stones, much less when they are wet and slippery. But that condition didn't slow me down – nor my assailant. I literally chewed up the multiple steps leading up to Goodwill, scaling them by twos and threes, but my pursuer was just as equal to the task. (What fuelled his determined drive? It must have been his blown stereo amplifier. He must have spent a fortune on it.)

But then I was running for my home, my second place of refuge. I barely had time to enter my mother's house when I heard the cutlass cutting wind behind my head. He respected my mother's house; I breathed a sigh of relief. But it must have taken a lot of self-control to resist the temptation to invade our privacy. And you should have heard the man breathing fire and brimstone and kicking dust outside like a mad bull.

"If you is a man, come back outside!" he shouted.

Wanting to prove that I was a man enough, I went to my room and got what I wanted – a .38 special. (At this point in time I will not reveal how I got to be in possession of it.) And proceeded to the front door. My mother tried her best to prevent me from going outside to have this – er – showdown. But I am extremely hard-headed, and so I didn't allow her to restrain me (I knew what I was about).

When I opened the door, the guy had the cutlass making sparks on the road surface. He started saying, "In your mother..." But when he recognised what I had in my hand, his eyes widened.

"Finish say what you was going to say there, nuh?!" I challenged him.

Instead of doing so, he turned about and fled for his life without uttering another word. Bystanders started screaming, "Murder! Police!" and running out of my potential line of fire as well. I chased the guy, laughing inside (soon you'll know why). It was clear that he was now twice as fast than when he was chasing me (he was firing on all eight cylinders!).

As we reached an intersection, guess who we met? How you know that so good? You've hit it. It was the police (CID) in their patrol car. The guy was extra glad! He embraced the "silver bullet", the CID's silver Toyota and, naturally, I gave up the chase. But when the cops sized up the situation, saw the gun in my hand, the mad gesticulation and heard the erratic speech of my ex-pursuer , they commanded: "Hey boy, come with that gun you have there." I knew that I was "safe", but knowing how uneducated and unpredictable some cops can be, I decided to give them a run for their money.

(Yes, oui.) The four CID personnel got out of their transport and gave chase (they maybe thought it was an unlicensed firearm). So there I was again, in the thick of the action, this time playing hide and seek with four CID agents.

After dodging and faking them for some time, I jumped a gate that had something written on it in red paint (I didn't have time to make it out). I touched down in the person's yard, twisting my right ankle. As I lay there on the ground, nursing my injury, I wondered why the cops had not pursued me there. I got the answer right away. I heard a dog barking and it was coming in my direction. Now it was clear that there had been some sort of "warning" written on the gate. At a glance, the dog looked like a wolf – no need to say, I was on my feet again like lightning! No kidding! I sprinted the 25 or so yards to the far fence in zero point zero seconds (Ben Johnson with all his steroids couldn't see me! The sprained ankle was the furthest thing from my mind.) When I reached the fence, a six footer, it was touch and go. I was up and over in a flash. And crash-landed in the next lane, like a plane, and there my injury – and the cops – caught up with me.

"Now let us have the firearm!" they demanded.

"Which firearm?" I asked innocently, rising up.

"The one you were chasing the man with."

Limping, I presented it to them from inside my belt – it was my nephew's toy gun – and stated: "A toy gun, oui." The cop in command said that it was still an offence to threaten anyone with a toy gun. Holding my now swollen ankle, I countered, "But he threatened me with a real cutlass."

The guy who had chased me so relentlessly stuck out his tongue for me (like the big child that he was) and said provokingly, "They going to charge you doh! BEEAA!" I stood up and pointed in the direction of Roseau and answered, "Yes, and you have a traffic ticket waiting for you, where you park it in the middle of the road." That brought him back to reality. How much they charge him? I doh know! What happen to my case? It doh call yet!

So. drivers be discreet when you drive, especially when it is raining, because the next pedestrian you might wet might just be me! And you know what will happen, I will certainly wet you back.

IN MONTEGO BAY

After reading in a newspaper about the adventures of a brave reporter who made a daring daylight drug purchase in Montego Bay, as we call that part of Newtown, I decided to see for myself what really transpires behind the drug scene. Armed with the newspaper article, I ventured to do my own investigation. Who tell me to do that? Some might be saying, "That good for you!" Anyway, let us go on with the story.

Well, to begin with, I had a number of options as to where to do my "illegal" purchase. In my newspaper's report was a list of all the popular outlets – Wall Street, Twenty Four Seven, the "Hole" Gutter, Baytown, Baghdad, Montego Bay etc. I chose Montego Bay. Why? Because this was where the "Rambo" reporter had her experience, plus she stated that the transaction went like a "piece of cake", and besides I had an alibi – the place where I usually buy my favourite bread is next door. So I felt quite safe in this habitat.

As I approached the bread depot, a "hustler" that I was accustomed to confronted me and asked: "Give me a couple of coins to check a scene nuh?"

"On condition," I said to him, "that you do something for me."

"What is that?" he demanded.

"All I am asking for," I answered, "is a 100% piece of rock." He raised his eyebrows in surprise. "Aye, aye, you in that too then?"

"So long..." I replied.

He then asked how much rock I wanted. "Ten, twenty, thirty or forty piece?" I said that I would settle for a "forty dollar piece", like the brave reporter did when she went on her assignment.

So I gave the guy two purple 20 EC dollar bills and off he went on his "mission". I waited and waited but, to my dismay, the guy never showed up. "He take you!" a bystander commented. But all was not (yet) lost because I knew that I would run into him again before long because I was accustomed to this character and he often hustled me for change to "bad up" his head.

And sure enough the very next day I ran into him unexpectedly, after purchasing my daily bread. "What you tried on me yesterday boy?" I asked him in a rough way.

"But I had come oui... Where you had go nuh?" he asked, putting on an act. He was lying, I knew it.

"What happen? Is like you go for it right in St Lucia, man." I countered.

"Who told you?" he replied. "I didn't know you was really serious, but doh dig, you doh lose your money, you know, I will set you up good. I coming." He motioned me to wait.

I did. This time he came back, a little late but better than never. And to my surprise he delivered my "silver pack" to me right there on the spot, under the telephone post, by the road with so many passers-by in the noon-time blazing sun. I got nervous on the spot. My knees felt wobbly and I could hardly walk.

"What if police hold me now?" I asked him.

"Just put that in your mouth man," he replied, cool like a

cucumber. I did as he suggested. My fear was at its heights now because I had heard on the radio about so many instances where people had died after ingesting drugs. I could not wait to reach the safety of home.

Somehow, only God knows, I made it home to my den and commenced opening my enticing "pack". I just had to see what this scourge was all about. After opening the foil with somewhat trembling hands, it appeared that I had already seen the contents somewhere before. After in-depth analysis I discovered that it was in deed and in fact candle wax. That just could not be the "Rock" of Gibraltar that was causing all this commotion in our society. I was totally disappointed. But I just couldn't leave it at that.

Right away, I returned to my place of purchase and searched out the culprit to make him understand that his ploy didn't work. "What the hell you think?" I roared. "You take me for a big donkey or what? If I had wanted $40 worth of candles I would have gone to the shop."

"Cool it, cool it, take it easy," he mumbled. "I will bring the real thing for you. But you really in it then?"

"That I telling you so long," I told him, trying to cover my tracks. "You see, I am an undercover smoker." He disappeared and I crossed my fingers expecting the worst. But this time he reappeared with lightning speed. But before I could receive my delivery, I got a blessing in disguise. Guess what?

Behind me, I heard a terrifying screech of a vehicle braking suddenly. When I turned to investigate the cause of the excitement, I identified the vehicle instantly. It was the dreaded drug squad pick-up truck. And yes, you guessed it, they were making a raid on the boys of Montego Bay.

I don't have to tell you. Instantly, I became a nervous wreck. I got cold sweat and my heart was doing a hundred and add beats per second. Man, I was trembling like a leaf. When I turned again to assess my contact, it was just in time to see him flick the silver foil pack into his mouth and down it went, I suppose.

What else do you expect? I got a complete "search down" from head to toe. To say the least, I was relieved when that episode was over. One of the police officers asked me, "What were you doing here?" "I... I... I... am a... a... a... a.... re.. re.. reporter," I stammered. He gave me a weird look and said, "Reporter my ace!" Then he ordered, "Move from there!" I quickly evacuated the area; I didn't stay around to witness the final outcome of the raid. I said to myself, "To hell with that $40, never me again."

But you doh hearing nuh? Since that time, the guys in Montego Bay are watching me as a police informer, oui. A sell out! They thought I was hand in glove with the drug squad and had tried to "set them up". And the worst part is ever since that close encounter in Montego Bay, the cops have been watching me suspiciously, like I really into drugs oui! Clearly, the newspaper reporter was much more lucky than me.

THE INTRUDER

I had left my aged mother's home unattended that Friday afternoon. She had gone to our home village to spend some days with relatives so I returned after sundown to switch on the lights (to deter would be burglars) so that I could return to continue playing dominoes at the club house. But it appeared that an intruder had already made an entry for the lights were on. It also appeared that the person was utilising my amenities at random: kitchen stove, blender, television and sound system (this last one my mother doesn't know how to operate).

Not wanting to take the law into my own hands, I ran over to the closest public telephone booth and called the police. The switchboard operator put me onto CID who, to my dismay, said that they would come only when and if transportation was available.

I put the receiver down abruptly and cursed under my breath. Then suddenly I got a bright idea. So I dialled again and pretended to be an anonymous caller who had some information on a "drug man". I gave the directions to my home in urgency and, believe me, before I could replace the receiver the drug squad had arrived. Hear them: "Where him? Where him?" I told them that in fact a burglar was in my house. When they heard why I had deceived them (I not lying), they just sucked their teeth, re-entered their drug van, slammed the doors and gave me a stern warning, saying, "Don't you ever try that again!" and drove off. Just so!

So what I did? I decided this time to take the law – and also a piece of 2 x 4 wooden stick – into my hands and stealthily entered our home like a cat stalking its prey. I could see that the intruder had indeed "made himself at home". You know what else? When I came to my room and peeped through the keyhole, I saw that the culprit was sleeping on my bed. I said to myself, "Them thieves getting more bold and brave."

Thus I kicked open the door determined to give my bed a serious beating! But luckily the sleeper spun around and I got a glimpse of his features in the nick of time (but because of my predetermined plan he still got a glancing blow). I stayed with my jaws agape, and froze in after-action.

It was a notorious cousin of mine from south, who was a character of some sort. He carried a number of aliases, like Batman, Crazy Glue, McGyver, Sticky Fingers, Lightening, Outlaw and Ninja Man to name a few. He quickly got up from the bed and said, "What happen to you nuh? You just hitting me like that... and close your mouth, before it ketch some flies."

I remained speechless because the stories that I had heard about him had made me wary of him. And he was the last person I was expecting to meet at my home. He loved OPP (other people's property), that is the reason why times before whenever he came to our house, I would just pay him off so that he could leave before he helped himself to some of our stuff. (He just couldn't leave people things alone.)

Rumours say that he is on to drugs hence his "touching" problem, and he is very good at it. Once, he entered a business place downtown and as soon as the proprietor saw him enter, he ordered all his employees and security personnel to quit whatever they were doing and place Ninja Boy (I call him boy because he is still in his teens) under full-time surveillance. They did, but you doh hearing, he still "take them" oui. The next time he made an appearance at the business house, the owner paid him a $100 bribe just so that he wouldn't enter his premises.

But, another time when he was in the vicinity, I misplaced my wallet fully loaded with various currencies. After a fast and frantic search I found it exposed on the couch in our drawing room. I counted the money over and over and over again and found none to be missing. I confronted him for an explanation, because that wasn't the norm. He confessed that he thought I was "testing" him, therefore he resisted the temptation. It was a good thing he did, oui.

So now, I asked him, "What you doing here?" He answered: "Aye, aye, you get your voice back?" and continued, "I wanted by the police, they have some warrants out for me, so I just want a little rest up till I get some money to go Guadeloupe." I warned him early in advance, "I doh have money!" "Is OK," he replied. "If I wanted to mess you up, I would just take what I want in your house and move."

"Tell me something," I said, "Where you pass to come inside there?" (There was no sign of a forced entry.) He told me, "A vòlé like me! There is no way you could hide your keys anywhere around the house for me not to get it!"

So just being curious I then asked him how did he intend to raise the funds to pay his back-door passage. He replied casually, "Doh fraid for me. By the time I make a couple rounds around Goodwill and I will be well set up."

If it weren't for my Bible studies, I would have told him in no uncertain terms that he would immediately have to go. But when I am knocking on heaven's door, I didn't want for the good Lord to turn me away as well, saying to me in effect (Matthew 25:42): "I (God) was hungry and you did not feed me; a stranger (cousin) and you refused me hospitality; in prison and you did not visit me; a thief and drug addict and you didn't help me out etc." Plus, I saw the potential of a good story for me – and you – in terms of informatics on safety tips in and around your home in these (unpredictable) days.

I settled down and sourced some data from Ninja Boy. How does he go about selecting his targets? He said, "When it comes to vehicles, I choose those without alarms and those with 'darkers'; and for houses, I go for those without occupants, or, if the residents are at home (at night), I select those with video and TV, especially those viewing cricket."

I asked him for an explanation on the latter. He reasoned, "Dominica have plenty TV people; they virtually live in front of their TVs and most of them wouldn't know that a stranger is in their home with them until he steals the TV."

"But you making it sound easy man!" (I had to confess.)

"You doh believe me, come and see tonight."

I couldn't believe that he really had the audacity to prove his point. He brought me by a certain house in upper Goodwill. I posed up under a lamp post – mark you, I was not his look-out man. While he said, "Watch that, I going and take the tape deck in mister house," he disappeared in the darkness. Fifteen minutes later, he returned with the tape deck plus a couple of cassettes. I said, "Doh lie, you and him have a connection, he give it to you!" "No man," he replied, "my victim's eyes were glued to his TV although I throw down a cassette he still doh take me on. He was watching a true blue movie."

Next thing, Ninja Boy telling me to "rest" the tape deck by me till he get a sale for it! I told him, "But, apart from being a big vòlé, you mad too!" He realised that that aspect was out of the question. So he took his "item" and went about his business.

About an hour or so later, he returned with some black notes ($100 bills) and some purple ($20 bills) and boasted that it went like "hot bread". I reasoned to myself, "Whether you are God or not, sooner or later you will bring police in my house!" Hence, I pleaded with him to make his stay as short as possible. He replied, "I can understand the scene, doh dig uncle [I am not his uncle]. When I come back from the 'Loupes', I will bring something nice for you."

I answered, "No thanks." I had heard too many stories about French people and their obeah capabilities.

BLOCK 44

What I go and do in the infamous Block 44 all the way in Grandbay? It is a long story, but I will try and make it short.

What happened is an old friend from schooldays invited me to come up for Isidore, the annual village feast. I really didn't want to go. I had heard too many negative stories about "Grandbayrians". Therefore I told my friend, "I good where I is!" But it had been a long time that he had been constantly asking me to visit and I couldn't continue to put it off. So I said, "OK. I will come, but you have to give me protection".

"You too stupid! They cannot touch you," he replied. He even went as far as to say, "When you come, just ask anybody for me and that is your passport. Everybody know me good and once is me you come to, you safe." I didn't believe him because I know that talk is cheap, but I still took him up on his offer.

Yes oui, I went up by bus. The ride on the bus is a story by itself. Them busman driving so fast! But what that concerned me the most was that the drivers have only two deadly options: to hit a cliff or to take a plunge into a precipice. It was a good thing we took none and therefore arrived safely. The bus "put me down" (like our typical bus drivers, in the middle of the road, like he owned it and my first impression was of the beautiful women all over the place. But I kept my tail quiet. I didn't want to offend anybody. I was fully aware that I was a stranger in "Sout City".

I met another "old friend". "Boy long I doh see you. What

you doing here garçon?" he asked. I bought him a Kubuli beer and described the purpose for my visit. When I mentioned my other friend to him, he said that "he" (my original friend) was indeed popular and well known by all in the village. He told me, "Just go on Block 44, he bound to be there. If he not there, he coming just now."

I proceeded to the infamous Block, but before arriving there I diversified my money, putting some in each pocket so that it would not appear that I was loaded. I didn't want to tempt a "bad head". An old saying of my grandfather's registered in my head, "If you want your neighbour to be honest, lock your doors." Basically, don't tempt no one. I was not afraid that the police would meet me there because it is standard knowledge that Block 44 is a "no go" zone for police patrols. Whenever they dared to pay a visit, they had to go fully armed with plenty reinforcements.

So there was I on "Block 44" live and direct. I didn't see my friend on the block but decided to approach a bar in the interior of the block. To do that I had to pass through a human alley of rough tops, big dreads and also a couple crazy bald heads. That was a challenge for me, but I braved the situation. I saw guys doing their own thing, some were smoking, rolling out, buying, selling and so on. After I had bypassed a couple of them, one individual challenged me. He "jacked" me in the neck and chest area and asked, "Where is your licence for coming here?" Without really thinking but not wanting to appear scared, I "jacked'"him in return, and said, "That is my passport!"

That reaction "freaked" them out. I heard somebody else

say, "Tax the man!" Apparently he was referring to some sort of Block 44 "user fee". Maybe I should have said who I was looking for, first thing first, but as it happened my mouth was faster than my brain, so I blurted out, "You parro man?!" (That is, are you a crackhead?) That statement must have ignited something in his head. The guy flared up in a rage. "Parro, I parro! What you say? I parro!" I never knew he would have taken it this way. It appears that was the worst thing I could have said.

This brings to mind an excerpt from Proverbs 18:6-7: "A fool gets into constant fights. His mouth is his problem! His words endanger him." My opponent made a lunge at me. I didn't back down. It was too late! Although I am not the fighting type, I thought this was the time to fight fire with fire (especially since I know a little bit of martial arts after years of watching Bruce Lee movies). So I stepped aside and blocked his punch and let him have a big "right" of my own. That stopped him in his tracks, bust his lips and sent him staggering backwards.

I saw the rest of the guys encircle me. A couple of them held some beer bottles menacingly in their hands. I knew they could become devastating weapons. A thought flashed through my mind. It appeared that I would be going back down to Roseau on a stretcher. But I was pleasantly surprised when I heard my opponent say to the others, "Doh come in it, is me and mister alone." Thus we engaged in serious combat. As we exchanged blows, I knew I could not count on the police to rescue me.

Eventually, we got burnt out (especially I, after throwing

some punches that missed their target completely) and the fight stopped of its own accord. Nobody intervened. We were out of breath and could only watch each other, breathing heavily like two heavyweight boxers in their twelfth round.

I thought the fight was about to recommence (round two) when the guy raised his hand. I put up my guard, but no blow came. Instead, it was an affectionate pat on the shoulders. I was taken aback. "Yes," he said, "you prove yourself today, my boy! You not a scout but a soldier! Come and drink a Kubuli on me."

Well yes, after that brawl the cold Kubuli was just what I needed. The first round of drinks was on his account (I do not know how he makes his living) and I claimed responsibility for the second and somebody else sponsored the third, and so on. It was like I was being initiated into a special society.

Later, my ex-opponent said that I gave a good account of myself and that from now on, if he should come across anybody or any group of persons messing around me, he and the rest of the guys from Sout City would be my allies and bodyguards and also that the olive branch was being held out to me on Block 44 to time indefinite.

"They" said jokingly that I was second only to the parliamentary representative (what a turn around). I was promised by the boys on the block that the next time I would be visiting Block 44, I would get the "red carpet" treatment and a 21-gun salute!

You doh hearing? After all that had been done and said, it's then my original friend turning up and he telling me, he come from checking a scene oui! After I done get my baptism on Block 44.

THE DINNER

But can you imagine me at an official dinner? Come on! All functions that I had previously attended were unofficial. The attire was usually informal and that meant for me strictly blue jeans. So, use your creativity and imagine me in a jacket and tie suit, and at an official dinner at that.

But let me make it clear, I like to eat. My girl usually call me a "greedy something". But that doesn't mean that I am a big belly man. My mother always asked me, "Where your food does pass nuh?" It seems it goes into my feet (size 12 inches).

So, as an aspiring writer, I was invited to this dinner, but also invited to contribute $100. Reluctantly I paid, but before Dinner-Day arrived, I went on a 24-hour hunger strike. Why? Because I wanted to eat my $100 worth of food. Imagine, that day, my stomach was saying "Beiok" regularly. So when the sun set I was more than ready to end my fast.

The night came and I put on my Sunday best. When my girl saw me, she asked if I was going to masquerade or carnival "jump up". But I didn't take her on, she maybe was just jealous. I had no problem with that. I just wanted to full my belly. Well, she looked proper and made up for any deficiency I may have had in my dressing.

But when we arrived at this high-class hotel, I really felt out of place. Even my transport felt ashamed – it broke down and stalled. The vehicles were top of the line cars: strictly V6s Cressidas, Pajeros, Legends, Altimas, Accords, Crowns etc and personnel to match.

I was regretting that I did not follow the advice of my girlfriend about taking a crash course in table mannerism. But I thought "to hell with that, I there already!"

When I saw the setting of the table, I remembered the time there was a party held by one of the high schools and we (ragamuffins) came to "crash it" and were turned away. So we made a conspiracy and stole the "bom" of food (a peleau) and blows fell on the chicken alone – nobody wanted the rice. Those were the (excuse me) good old schooldays. So I toyed with the idea of making another "mission impossible" possible but this time only in my head.

We got seated around the long table, my girl was on my right (I could tell she was nervous, "afraid" for me). Every now and then she would advise me on the proper procedure. I observed the attitude of some of the participants (nose in the air types) and got the impression that they were made of glass or some other precious material, and did not descend from the sinful Adam and Eve line.

But when I perceived that the dinner course was about to begin, my mind registered on my marks, get set… go…Pow! Hence I helped myself and ever so often, I would knock a glass or some other bit of chinaware. Whenever I did, I would glance around our table to see the reaction of the other players. When our eyes would clash, I would get this unspoken reaction, "Who is that unmannerly pig?" I sensed the impending disaster, but hoped for the best.

There were dumplings (joe boys) on the menu and that is an old country favourite of mine. I rubbed my belly in anticipation and managed to get some on to my plate with the help of a big spoon. So now I was ready to devour, but then came the main problem. I have to use knife and fork. Therefore, I had the knife in my right hand and the fork in my left hand as recommended.

But I am a right hander and I'm accustomed to using a mono instrument at home, the fork, and I am very versed with the fork in my right hand. I do everything with the fork, crush, eat, "demeatise" (separating the meat from bone) and so on, and if I should encounter any difficulties I can always count on good old fingers.

I beat around the bush with the other ingredients in the dish but I was marking the dumplings, so I made a prod with the fork (an exploratory probe) but the dumpling eluded the fork. I "chuke" it again and once more the troublesome dumplings evaded the fork. I looked around uneasily to see who was observing that contest.

My girl was the only observer, she nudged me in the rib with her elbow. So I diverted and decided to take an appetiser, that is, a whisky. I took two in a row, but I wanted to eat my hundred dollars worth of food. Hence, I resumed my attack on the joe boys, but they were as elusive as ever. It was difficult for me to execute that manoeuvre and keep my composure and elbows in position as required by etiquette. In another attempt, my fork struck a sour note in my plate after a near miss, and all eyes fell on me. I returned a plastic smile to all and reverted to my drink.

After some time I decided it was a do or die situation and I took a chance and gave the dumpling one juke! And missed again. The dumpling "pitched" on the tablecloth. The event commanded the attention of all. I grabbed the dumpling with my bare hands and said to it, "Only here you can do that!" and put it into my mouth (there was no escape for it now). You should have seen the look I got from the majority of spectators but some just laughed. My chick whispered, "Nobody will invite you to even a picnic again!" I answered, "So what? I doh care!" and reverted to my usual "home style" of eating. I had to make up for lost time.

I made myself at home and started to put blows on the food chain. I let the bones make powder like a big dog. Some high-ups stared in astonishment, others in amazement. But they soon realised that I was enjoying myself to the full, and some followed my cue, putting aside their codes of ethics and principles, they pitched in. Others reluctantly dug in as well. I didn't care about their reservations because I know most are like pigs (at home) but put on false fronts. And I was determined not to let respect of humanity to allow me to starve to death!

When I was through, I was filled almost to my ears, I let out a gigantic belch and said, "Yes, I ram now!" tapping my bulging stomach. My girl in disgust stamped her high heels on my big toe. I shouted "AAAAIIIEEEEE"... everybody looked in my direction. As a cover up, I stood up and continued, "... want to make a toast". The drinks had gone to my head.

I held up my drink and commenced: "Here's to you... for as good as you are and as bad as I am, I am still as good as you are… as bad as I am...!" I got a round of applause.

For weeks after I was the star of the dinner, but I am yet to get another invitation. That is true.

THE CHASE

Some might get the impression that I enjoy being on the wrong side of the law. But it is not really my fault. I do try to do "good" and I usually end up getting bad instead. Like, for instance, on this occasion.

I was coming down from the countryside after a hard day's work (it was about 8.30 pm) with my rather aged transport, one of the popular Japanese types. I was just cruising in no hurry.

I saw this guy looking stranded. He had with him a medium-sized parcel, and he asked for a ride. Trying to be a good Samaritan, I gave him a lift (because I know how difficult it is to get a ride at these times). He didn't speak much as we drove to town. He was seated next to me in the co-pilot's seat and I didn't ask him what he was "selling" either. Basically, I was uninterested.

I was enjoying the music being played on my radio when I rounded a bend and saw a figure moving across the road. My reflex was a bit slow because he was dressed in camouflaged battle fatigues. He was "hard to see"; he lucky, I nearly jam him! I realised he was a cop. He motioned me to stop. I was about to comply when my passenger said, "If you stop, you in trouble! Trust me!" I queried, "What you mean?" He said urgently, "I have ganja on me!"

It was then the truth struck. The parcel he was carrying was laced or maybe I should say loaded with narcotics. I panicked and "reflex" got the better of me. I didn't want my old faithful to get seized. It was common knowledge that vehicles caught involved in the drug trade usually got impounded. So there it was...

At the time I was slowing in a third gear, automatically I selected a lower gear, second, and pressed the accelerator pedal to the metal and released the beast. In street talk, we call that a "race change". As I pulled away at maximum revs, I let go the third gear and glanced into the rear-view mirror and saw the lights of a vehicle just being switched on (it must have been hidden in the bushes), but I knew I had a lead on them. I flicked in the fourth gear and then the fifth.

And my boy, you doh hearing! The "old jalopy" never know it could run so! (I really believe that age is just a number.) Imagine, it was night time and I never slowed for any oncoming vehicles. It didn't matter how bright their headlights were. I was trying my utmost best to keep the cops at a distance. I didn't want them to see my tail lights at all!

Hear that. But when I downshifted and rounded a popular corner and hill, the vehicle made a 90 degree turn (it was across the road!). Using all the skills available, I steered it back on course and into the climb. The "guilty party", seeing the drama and excitement and James Bond-type stunts being played out "live" (his nerves maybe gave way) told me, "Stop! Stop! Stop! Put me down!" (But knowing that time was crucial, stopping was out of the question.) I ignored him and thought to myself, "You going to hell with me."

After some seconds, I asked him to monitor how far behind they were (at the speed I was driving, I couldn't dare take my eyes off the road). One would have thought that I was travelling on a straight road. Why? Because I took all corners and bends, big or small under full throttle. The tyres were protesting and screaming. (I have never driven that fast before nor since.)

The "stranger" told me that the cops were still coming but were not gaining on me, as a matter of fact he said that I was "stretching" them, extending my lead. That was welcome news; it suited the "secret" plan that I had formulated in my head. I was 100% conscious that I was approaching a "certain village" that is well known for having unpredictable traffic jams (it and it little neighbour). I knew that it would be pure suicide to enter that village with the drug hunters in hot pursuit. Therefore I was prepared to take all risks to implement that plan.

At a certain spot I made an abrupt almost 180° degree turn around and immediately turned off my headlights and navigated by "radar" a track (off road) that I knew so well (like the back of my hand) that I could negotiate it in total darkness, but "slowly".

That "piece of work" gave the cops the slip. It must have appeared to them that the "ride" had disappeared into thin air. I knew that they were counting on "ketching" me stuck in a road block in that troublesome village (traffic-wise), but thanks to experience I was one step ahead that time.

(You know I believe up to this present day that the drug squad are still scratching their heads and wondering, "What on earth happened on that eventful night?")

When I finally stopped and turned off the ignition, the engine was overheating and belching hot water and steam.

The "stranger" breathed a sigh of relief when he heard the police van racing pass (voom!) on a wild goose (or wild ghost) chase. He turned to me and shook my hand and gave me a high-five. I wanted to thump him for putting me at risk but a little bit of sense prevailed. In acknowledgement, he said, "You lucky you know how to drive good, you plenty better than the average drivers." I asked him, "Who lucky me or you?" With a grin he said, "Both of us, oui."

He then apologised for the inconvenience he caused. When he offered me a cut in his illegal stuff as compensation, I just said, "Noooo thank you!"

DE JAM

INA

It was a long time since I had been to a jam. So some might believe I am more or less a home boy, who would just stay home and watch TV. And they are almost very right in their suspicions, though sometimes it is the other way around – where I would suddenly wake up in the middle of the night and find it was the TV that was watching me!

So, well, my employer wanted me to find out why there were so many violent incidents at places where the idea was to have clean fun. So after a long absence from these activities, I was to make a comeback. I had kept my distance because I found a number of persons would come to these jams with knives instead of money in their pockets, and some were more willing to use tear gas instead of air fresheners or deodorant to clean the sweaty atmosphere. Plus, when one listens to the directions to the choreograph of dances in the songs being played, it's almost always – a push somebody, slap somebody, kick somebody and if you are not a "ruff neck" go on the side etc.

So whenever I would go out, it was always a cool session and a one-on-one affair with one of my three "faithful" partners. I grade them according to favoritism: No 1, No 2 and No 3 (You understand?). Naturally No 1 is my favourite and No 2 is a standby and when for some strange reason "they" (No 1 and No 2) start acting up, No 3 could always take in the slack.

I did not tell none of "my people" about by latest assignment. I told them separately that I would not be going to that specific "big jam". (I wanted to avoid being accused of conflict of interest.)

So yes, I went to the jam and posed up outside, observing people attitude for the first 90 minutes. And it was obvious to me that some partygoers (not much, you know) didn't come to have a good time but rather to fight; they were like time bombs, just waiting for their fuses to run out. And even when I try to be polite to them – saying things like, excuse me and please – they would glare at me like I had done something out of the way. But anybody can be a "ruff neck" once you throw caution to the wind!

Well, I went into the dance hall, and strolled over to the bar to wet my throat. People were getting drunk and high and couples were stroking back and stroking forth here, there and everywhere on the dance floor. After having one or two drinks – it maybe was more – I started to feel flirty, and I noticed a young lady who activated my sensuality, so I made "a pass" (try something nuh?) like in my younger days.

Boy, who tell you? The girl watched me like I was less than a dog, silently saying in effect, "How dare you?! Mash!!" I kept my cool (I am no fool), her man was probably close at hand. But when I glanced at the entrance of the door of the jam, I saw my No 3 enter, that made me feel much better. I went back and told the "slut": "You making as if 'your thing' make out of gold!" And turned to my big mampy and started stroking away.

My mampy told me, "I didn't know you would be there."

"Me neither!" I replied.

While dancing, I explained that I was merely mixing work with pleasure, just for this assignment. Then something weird happened. Out of the corner of my eye, I caught a glimpse of my No 2 also making an entry. I hastily made an excuse and said that I had an inconvenience and was going to the lavatory.

I saw the real possibility of hostilities escalating if I should be caught in a cross-fire between No 2 and No 3. So I sneaked out of the dance-floor area. A so-called friend of mine who saw the way I was acting got suspicious and asked, "Police looking for you nuh?..." I told him I didn't have time to explain, and asked him to occupy my No 2 while I made myself scarce.

It worked (for a while). I went outside and pondered on my next move.

While resting on a vehicle parked outside in the semi-darkness, somebody grabbed me from behind and covered my eyes and said, "Guess" (Who?). You doh hearing?! It was my favourite: No 1. Well, I had some more explaining to do. While trying to talk my way out of this situation without making matters worse, we gradually got aware that a fight was in progress in the dance hall. Next thing, I seeing the so-called friend coming outside and searching me out. Before I could ask him what was going on, he said urgently, "Come and stop them two woman you bring there! They fighting!"

That put me in a real fix. I watched my girl's face searching for advice. "Go and stop them, nuh!" she said (in a hard-to-explain way) and turned her back (on me). Not knowing how I was going to do it, I returned to the dance floor where the fight was in high gear (at its heights).

Now I had a serious dilemma. (I used to wonder why people were so reluctant to intervene in fights of this nature, it always appeared that the "peacemaker" usually get the worse of the outcome, unless he or she can beat up the two fighters put together.) I knew No 3's fighting potential first hand (she was a big-body girl). Once, trying to get her not to walk alone too late at night, I staged a mock mugging. While she was approaching her home one night, I jumped out of hiding (well, masked up like a ninja) and said, "Stick it up!" She asked boldly, "Where's your gun?" I answered, "It in my pants."

Boy, before I could gather my wits, she hit me over the head with her purse. I doh know what she had in it, but it swelled my head. It must have been her cell. Next she kicked me on the shin – that hurt as well. I realised that I was in for trouble. I was forced to own up and quick! "Me 'at there! Me 'at there!" I repeated in quick succession. She told me, "You lucky! I was going and kick you somewhere else." "I know that!" I said.

So there she was in full glory taking advantage of my deputy, who, naturally, was no match for her. Reluctantly, I decided to grab her from behind to get her off my second in command. As I approached, I got a backlash from a Soca bottle she had in her hand to disfigure No 2 who was slightly better-looking than her. I didn't abandon the strategy and held on. No 2 seized that opportunity of the lull in the onslaught to retaliate. She picked up a chair and using all the power she had left, swung it (full force!). No 3, being a champion girl, just shifted me in its path (I should have "let go"). When it slammed into me, I felt as if all the bones in my fragile body were fractured! When some other so-called acquaintances saw that I was getting nowhere and also getting the worst of it, they intervened to my welcomed relief. Praise God!

But for the next couple of days, I was the talk of the town. Every Tom, Dick and Harry, Jane and Mary was saying, "He playing 'big dan' and have three woman he cannot control."

I now realise that a number of other factors can contribute to violence in these jams. Now is like they give me a "stay home dumpling". I doesn't go nowhere again (I serious).

MOST WANTED

Let me tell you: it was never my intention to blow my own trumpet, but if I don't blow it, who will? After all, it's mine! So now I have clarified that aspect.

Some persons known and unknown want me to entertain them with my down-to-earth and, most significantly, original stories. And because so much of the entertainment on television is foreign to our natural culture and heritage, there is a belief that products, services and things in general, made or done locally, are inferior to what's in the foreign market-place. Now you are reading these stories, you will have to agree that I have killed that myth, effectively, and for good! Do I have your support? (I should.)

And do you know, some persons that I confide in even commend me and say, "Boy, you good oui! – you really is a investigator and writer of class," and ask, "How do you do it?" (Well for now, that is my "top secret".) Some even suggest and propose new assignments for me to take on. They range from the bold and daring to just plain ridiculous and crazy. Like, for example, some put forward a behind-the-scenes look at how the white powder enters our nature isle, legally or illegally. Others say, investigate the rumours surrounding our infamous police inquiry. My answers are usually: "I know my limits!" And I do. Trust me.

And about some of the ridiculous missions? Some wives ask me to "surveillance" their husbands, to find out why their husbands stay (or pretend to stay) at work late, and when they come home, why they can't do their homework. And vice versa: some husbands ask me to find out what goes on at home, while they are sweating to earn, that make their spouses act like deep-freezes when they come home in a "good", excitable mood! Have they lost that loving feeling? But this kind of private detective work is not my kind of bag! Check somebody else.

And, as should be evident, I am certainly non-political. When election time comes around, I just go into the polling booth, and make my "X" at random – any port for a storm. But even with my neutrality, I still run into difficulties. Let me tell you something semi-political that occurred to me recently that caused me to realise just how badly I was really "wanted".

It was just last week, I was making the observation that Dominica is a very big island (to my small brain) because there are so many communities that are almost non-existent to me. It is like I could get lost in Dominica, like it was New York – you know what I mean? (I guess you do.) So, being and feeling adventurous, I decided to visit a certain unfamiliar hamlet on our north-west coastline and spend some bucks there.

I parked my old jalopy on the outskirts of the hamlet in question, and strode into that little village like a cowboy. It really felt so (I not joking – so why you giggling?). And it looked like a ghost town, except for a little child that I saw standing in a doorway, but who was soon violently pulled inside by unseen hands – and the door slammed shut! I started to feel self-conscious and paranoid. I heard the clumping sound of my footsteps rather profoundly and felt that numerous pairs of eyes were peering at me from behind blinds and through keyholes etc. I got the uncanny impression that the villagers were of a very shy disposition.

I heard some sporadic activity in the centre of the village and homed in on it. As I approached, something occurred that I didn't expect. Someone hollered out my code name. I frighten, but recognised the voice. It was someone who knew me exceptionally well, clearly.

And at that point some strange developments began to materialise – the residents commenced emerging from their various homes like zombies. For a minute, my imagination went berserk and I imagined the scenario to be that of a scary Hollywood thriller – and my heart started beating doop! doop! doop! doop. I thought they were coming out to strangle me! But all of a sudden the mood changed to the extreme opposite and I suddenly felt like a big-money movie star or president – or a prime mini-star mobbed by fans, well-wishers and the media etc.

What actually occurred is my partner had unwittingly blown the whistle on my true incognito identity because everybody commenced congratulating me and commending my work and asking question upon question, like I was some prime-time media star. They asked questions like: Have I been there? And done that? Trying to be brief, and straight to the point, I summarised it all, by saying: "My writings are more or less true lies." Are you with me? Imagine, some of the new crop of youth in the village even sought my autograph! And to really prove their reverence for me and my works some grown-ups offered to buy all my drinks – just like that!

Thus I entered the sole rum shop in the village and drinks

commenced going down in quick succession. But look the contrary part!

Suddenly, the happy talk took a drastic turn degenerating into politics. The debate quickly became intense. And, in the midst of it all, someone asked which political party I supported. I thought, "Damn!" and looked up to heaven (through the ceiling) and asked God a silent, "Why?!" So not wanting to displease any of my fans, I said like a big time Rastaman, "I-man, neutral seen!" A diehard supporter of a particular party wasn't pleased by my answer. Slamming a cutlass (I didn't see where it materialised from) on the counter, on its flat side, "Blawy!" he demanded, "Find a gear or else!"

Boy! Yes oui! I racked my mental gearbox and found a gear – it was full speed. Reverse! I needed immediately to get out of there so I made a quick exit, flying through the closest shop window and jumped on my "horse" (ie, my old jalopy) and sped away at full revs into the setting sun. So now you know why I keep so much of a low profile on politics.

JUNGLE RUN

I dare you to enter my world. You still there nuh? Oh, I see, you brave, then enter my time machine too nuh, and let us go back into time when I was younger (naturally) and back to the days of the "dread era" (the early 1970s) when we had gun-slinging dreads in the hills.

But how should I start? Well I, too, was then a member of an outlaw terrorist disorganisation, that is the dreads, who were wanted dead or alive for their dreadlocks and also for a number of slayings. But I was so young at the time that I was below suspicion, and so was able to play the role of courier for the "extremists" in the hills. I would bring them food supplies and tarpaulins for shelter, and some police information when obtainable. It was very risky but being a young outlaw I was able to perform.

But one day when I was down in the "Babylon" (the capital, Roseau), the police came upon a "camp" and a shoot-out ensued, which resulted in two dreads being shot dead. When the bodies were brought down to town, it was like an art exhibition – everybody was going to the mortuary to view the bodies. Can you remember? You didn't born yet?! What boy!

Anyway, I felt the loss because I knew those guys close – one on one. The other dreads had fled to another camp site in the heights of Belles, that I also had knowledge of. So, a couple of days after the shoot out, I visited the new camp, but it wasn't to a warm welcome. In fact, it was a very hot one because I was accused of being the informant who had disclosed the location of their camp to the police. I denied it but failed to convince the members of the deadly gang.

As a result, they beat me badly (boy, look blows!) and I was forced to eat hot pepper. At one point, they were going to rub some pepper in my eyes, and I knew – all too well – that I was on the verge of becoming another victim killed in the hills. In desperation, I attained extra strength and managed to wrestle free from my captors, and ran blindly into the surrounding jungle – like a "wild apache", with the "killer dreads" well-armed and dangerous in hot pursuit. The fire around my mouth was minor problems to the real fear in my heart – oh, how I wished I was down in Babylon!

Eventually, I found myself on the edge of a steep descent, which appeared to end in a sheer cliff drop to the famous Layou river way below. I was cornered, with my back to the precipice, and facing my potential executioners who were – I was now 100% sure – determined to kill me, like the others that I had witnessed getting their throats slit and shot before my very eyes. I knew just what I could expect. I heard the explosion of a shotgun and chose between death here and death below. Choosing the latter, I descended the steep slope, sliding and trying to grab tree stems to slow my descent. And last minute I found myself hanging precariously over the cliff and holding on to a small tree stem with little roots and no branches – for dear life. There was no way I could climb back up the virtually 90° slope – I looked down below me and saw the river blue/green and extra far – below. That was sure death to me.

I remembered the warnings of my mother – not to follow

bad company, and realised the truth of it, all too clearly now. I hope you don't have to have a similar experience to learn what I learned belatedly.

So there I was experiencing a real-life drama, "cliff-hanger" scenario. I heard the dreads talking above me – but the place was so deadly that they did not risk following, and decided, instead, to send some big stones down the slope, in an effort to finish me off. When I saw the boulders whizzing past me and my hands tiring, I called on my Heavenly Father and asked his forgiveness. I screamed, and screamed and screamed again (till I lost count) as the branchless stem decided to lose its roots and rooted out.

I must have blacked out, but gradually I became aware of a peculiarly burning sensation (it must have been the "sun splash" effect when I hit the water) and of being surrounded by ice-cold darkness. The cold feeling brought across the awareness that I was still very much alive! I looked up and saw light and quickly realised that I was in the depths of a deep gorge. I struggled desperately to reach the surface – and succeeded! But how! How else would this story be completed? Realising the height from whence I had fallen (Boy! It was high, oui!), I praised God realising he had performed yet another miracle.

I still was not out of the woods yet and I spent days roaming in the thick jungle trying to find my way back to civilisation, eating itals of all sorts for survival. Cold ground was my bed, rock stone was my pillow too. As the days passed, the jungle took on an appearance of an amazing maze and I began to hallucinate, and would see people but it was only figments of my imagination – I even thought that jumbie Beelzebub was taking hold of me. Eventually, I couldn't differentiate between reality and illusion. Imagine, I heard frogs barking and dogs croaking... Oh dear. Look, I'm getting all mixed up again – but I heard all kinds of strange sound effects. It was jungle madness – to me!

Until one day I got this awareness that I was in the hospital. The missing link is that I was found by villagers, delirious in the hills and was transported to this "human garage" institution, where after a number of days I made a recovery. Is true! Believe me.

But wait a while, I know you thought only Hollywood or Cinemax could give you that sort of entertainment – I'll be back! God willing.

CRICKET
LOVELY CRICKET?

To be quite honest, I am not much of a sport, nor, for that matter, much of a sportsman. But be honest (it's your turn), can you imagine me all in white and playing cricket – the gentleman's game? You can't? I knew that. Then allow me to tell you all about it.

Well naturally, I wasn't game about playing a so-called friendly cricket game (writers versus a village eleven) in this far country district. For one, I dislike the hardness of the cricket ball, and have little confidence in my reflexes at one score plus years. Hence, it took a lot of diplomacy and cunning on the part of a colleague to convince me to participate in this "gentleman's game".

I told my colleague, modestly, that I wasn't a Brian Lara or Courtney Walsh. Optimistically, he stated that, on the contrary, today I could be a Lara or Walsh easy because it was "easier yet" to score a duck! That statement did the trick, plus he said that I would get a long ride. To tell the truth, I got fed up with the ride – it was much too far.

Anyway, arriving in this mystery village, I realised that the game was destined to be very unusual when I saw the amount of liquor being abused by all persons – from umpire to spectators. I wouldn't lie – I didn't drink much because I didn't want to experience double vision and see two balls, and pay the penalty – get a bouncer!

The coin was tossed up and my captain's guess or ultimatum was correct. He told his counterpart, "Heads – I win, tails – you lose!" And his counterpart fell for it. That was my first witnessing of a "win win" scenario; my captain couldn't lose. So, I advised my captain, "Send them inside!" Let them bat first. I was hoping we could win without I having to make a batting contribution. Instead, he turned a deaf ear and opted for us to bat instead. Thus I asked to bat last – 10th man.

So "we" went in to bat, and cricket being the boring game that it is (to me), I soon dozed off until I was rather rudely awakened in the middle of a nice daydream by a teammate. "Wake up! Wake up! –just now you batting!" he said. I replied in a daze, "What?! Already!" And asked the score. It was a very meagre one (the actual number is not too important) – and it was for eight wickets, so we needed every run possible to make a fighting defence. I strapped on my pads and tried to get mentally prepared.

But the crux of our problem was (apparently) that the village team had a dream bowler of extra fiery pace – a crude version of Courtney Walsh! Boy! Look pace! When mister bowling, all you hearing the spectators saying is, "Wwheeee…" and "ooooHHHH…" and "AAAHHH" as the ball usually beat everybody – including the wicketkeeper. The only player who was showing any resistance was our captain. He was the only player in double figures – and not out yet. When the last batsman (before me) went, he was bowled all over this place. The ball went through him, the three wickets, the wicketkeeper and down to the boundary for four byes. That's an example of his pace.

Right away, I started to fear plenty more, and my knees smote each other as I strode out to the middle and my crease

– my boy! I was a "kapon" wreck, scared like hell! I patted the crease, but when I saw the length of the "run up" the bowler was utilising that broke my concentration. Half-way through, I broke his run up by straightening up and becoming "unready". The umpire signal "dead ball" and that infuriated the pace man. He cursed under his breath and returned for another run up (which was longer than the previously aborted one). At that point I shouted to the umpires: "Warn mister! If he hit me, I'll hit him back!" The square-leg umpire shouted, "The man have his ball to bowl and you have your bat. So defend yourself!" I warned, "I will make the bat turn into an offensive weapon, eh!" They paid me no mind.

Well, "my boy" (the Walsh) came down like a speeding bullet and jumped and delivered – I doh lying, I doh see the ball (up to now!). It was a blurr, but I attempted a blind stroke and felt a blow in my rib cage and abdomen that interrupted my breathing pattern. I doubled over and went down on my knees, like in prayer. The fieldsmen asked: "How's that?" The umpire said "Not out!"

But when my normal breathing pattern returned, I conceded and acceded. "I think, I out oui!" My captain came down the wicket and tried to encourage me to "stick it out". I said, "AHHWA! I retiring hurt." Trust me, the only reason why I did not hammer the bowler with the bat was because of the pain in my rib cage.

And that is how our innings folded – rather prematurely. But here's the next part of the story.

The villagers' cricket team went in to bat, and I made a remarkable recovery. How and why? Simply because I wanted revenge! But when my captain requested that I field close to the batsman, I refused point blank. I told him he was mad, and I was not that "silly" to field at silly mid on or mid off. Thus I opted for boundary fielding where I was very swift and businesslike in my approach. But I had two mishaps – once trying to cut off four runs, I unwittingly stepped on the ball and nearly broke my neck. The other time I was calm and cool waiting for a high ball to fall into my "safe" hands – but last minute the ball eclipsed the sun and blinded me. I just had time to turn my face and it hit me at the back of my head!

That aggravated my determination for revenge, and at last, it came, with my friend's turn to bat. Ha! That is what I was waiting for! Immediately I asked my captain for me to bowl. "But you is not a Walsh nor Ambrose nor Carl Hooper," my captain bemoaned. I told him, "Doh mind, I going to out him. Trust me!" I was extremely persistent and it worked, and I was handed the ball. Everybody wondered, what was happening. My "good friend" pointed to the boundary meaning he was going to hit me for six. I tried to bounce him and he did hit me for six! My captain said, "You see what I tell you." I replied, "Doh mind! Everybody does get hit for six every now and then, but I must out him!"

The next ball, I did not take much of a run. They must have thought I was going to try spin bowling, but before delivering, I planned my escape route, and pelted the ball like a baseball player – and out him in his rib cage – clean! He collapsed on the wickets, and I escaped the field of play. While everybody was looking for me, I was in town a long time ago!

But ever since, I have been living in fear of unexpected

retaliation – ever so often glancing over my shoulder. Then one day, in Roseau, when I was very complacent I was suddenly aware that my "antagonist" was approaching me. I doubted that he had seen me, but there was no escape. So, as a get away, I just lie down under a parked 4 x 4 truck (with my good clothes on!) like a roadside mechanic. Just to behold, he stopped alongside the ride to converse with somebody. At that moment, to put the icing on the cake, the driver entered his vehicle and started up.

I fly out from under the vehicle – and addressed my friend, "OK! OK! I sorry! Hit me back!" He responded, "Your '4ker'. I thought you would stay there…" And to my total surprise, he went on "Is all right man. I is a born again Christian (of a sort)." Man! I was relieved, I felt like a massive weight was taken off my shoulders .

"Thank you Jah! Rastafari!" I said with a sigh. And I have been contemplating becoming a Christian too, ever since. But I na ready yet, maybe when I am through writing my weird (but unique) stories. How about you? Are you ready?

T^{HE} KILLING SHED

Isn't it ironical and paradoxical that my imagination which is supposed to see me get food on my table can at times embarrass me at embarrassing times – like when I went up one weekend to my home village (guess which?) to look up my roots connections. On that particular voyage, I was accompanied by my future mate. She wanted to meet her in-laws (etc) and know the village of my birth much better. (I still not telling you its location or coordination.)

And a little after my initial arrival, nostalgically I sought solitude: to revisit some of my childhood haunts and to reflect on how much the times had changed and are continually changing. Taking a walk, with my thoughts, I eventually found myself by an old abandoned banana boxing plant, on the outskirts of our ecological village that had once boasted plenty activity when bananas were in full bloom. Gone are these days, like so many others...

So while chilling around and letting my memory roam, I heard two young men on the outside checking their scene. I guess they came around to smoke their "thing", whatever. And again, for some strange reason (I have probably told you already), I decided to play James Bond, my favourite "big screen" agent.

I didn't really want to hear what they were saying, but then again I didn't want them to know that a "secret agent" was in the area. Thus, I kept an invisible profile, enjoying the excitement of those covert actions. Most of what they said is not worth repeating except when their "talk" reached on a certain person's daughter that one of the young men stated he wanted "to kill". That pricked up my ears, more so, when I heard the other say, he wanted to "kill her" too. And to my total "blow brain", I heard them making detailed plans on how to perpetrate this (to my suspicious mind) gruesome crime.

Don't blame me on my imagination because we have all heard of the various arbitrary killings occurring in our once irie country. So there it was. I was making the link that as the young men had smoked this er "drug" (I doh know what it was), they were now contemplating (yet) another brutal murder!

Now, really, I didn't want to get involved, because I knew of a victim who had lost his life for so doing. But I did hear that they planned to lure the girl to this shed, that I at present occupied, the coming Sunday. I then thought it wise to get a glimpse of their features, and so spied them through the boards, and recorded their looks in my memory banks. Eventually, they left, and I left also, and returned to the village.

And, my friend, my head was hot! Very hot indeed! I really thought that I should just "mind my business" and shut my mouth trap. But my conscience bothered me – unrelentingly. So when my girl and I were alone, I related my story and fears for the young girl. My girl was totally indifferent to my suspicions of the schoolboys (that I learned they were after). She told me bluntly, "But for a big man you is a 'Da-mass' (a dam donkey), I doh know why I loving you?" I whispered, "…For the work", and she nearly knocked me out! But I told her that if anything negative should happen, I would not be able to forgive myself because I had foreknowledge. Thus she said satirically, "Well, call the police, nuh?... Mr Bond! James Bond!" I know she was ridiculing me, but I still thought it a good idea!

So I dialled, and gave the information, but the cops did not sound too enthusiastic to nip the "young criminals" in their budding stage. Instead, they asked my name. I was reluctant to give it, and so declined. But I asked again that they do something urgently. The officer on the other end of the line asked, "Do you drink?"

"No!" I replied.

He asked again, "You smoking crack?"

I asked in return, "Why you asking me that for?"

"That's because you're making a stupid report," came the reply.

Apparently, nobody was taking me seriously. I protested their lacklustre and unprofessional approach to crime prevention. To my dismay, the officer stated that they would respond only when the crime was actually committed – words to that effect, and hung up on me. (Have that ever occurred to you?) But when I related the outcome of my conversation with the cops to my girl, she said, "You see, you is a 'Da Mass'...I always telling you that?" I didn't answer, but I couldn't believe persons could be so apathetic in the midst of these insane occurrences in our nature isle.

However, I put these thoughts on the back burner. So Sunday came and I would have forgotten all about the pending crime, but – per chance – as I looked out of our country house, about midday, I saw one of the young men walking with this girl whom I (immediately) assumed was the potential victim. And a little after I saw the accomplice following a distance behind – had I not known of their plans, I would not have made the connection. So I called my girl, and excitedly relayed the latest developments. She looked at me with sardonic pity – that I couldn't understand at the time. But I told her that I was going to do something about it.

I thought that I could make a heroic move and maybe beat up the two "criminals" together. Reluctantly, my girl decided to come along. But I couldn't help noticing the sarcasm in her utterances whenever she got occasion to speak.

We followed the trio, at a distance. Naturally, it should be obvious, I was in the lead, while my girl with her I-couldn't-care attitude tagged along (she was holding me up). But I was still just in time to see the accomplice stealthily enter the banana shed's abandoned office.

Approaching the shed, I could hear the "crime" was already in progress. I heard some groaning, moans and some sharp cries. So, I watched my girl wondering if I should now break down the door like a "Rambo" and rescue the dame. She said in a low tone of voice, "What are you waiting for double '0' seven." I ignored her satire when I heard the "victim" cry out: "Stop! All you killing me! Oui, bon Dieu! Wooieee."

I prepared to kick the door open. But just before going into action, my girl held me back and said, softly, "A-soul. Before you pass like a donkey use the peephole!" I misheard, and so asked: "What 'people' have to do with it?" Then she pointed out the peephole to me. So strangely disoriented, I reluctantly peeped, and I doh know how to say it. But here they were, "killing", as it were, the person's child. It was embarrassing to the max again. My girl rubbed it in, "Do you agree?" But to find out what I saw – you will have to use your imagination, oui!

But then I am almost convinced that I must pull the plug (out) on my television or imagination and hang up my pen. What do you think?

FORBIDDEN ZONE

I was asked to do a report on the drug "hole" in the Gutter Village area. My friend, it might be true that I fancy myself as a James Bond, Mike Hammer, Magnum PI type investigator, but to speak the truth, I baulked. I told my boss, "If you doh like my head come out straight! It seems you see a six-foot deep hole in the cemetery for me, man." But it appears he used to be a top salesman before he took up his new job because he actually managed to coax me into giving it a go.

Remembering a past experience in a danger zone, I didn't want to embarrass myself again. So what I did? I decided to pay the inspector in charge of the drug squad a visit to secure immunity against accidental apprehension while on this special assignment.

So I entered the inspector's office and found it to be strangely dark. But he enlightened me when he said: "You can remove those sunshades you are wearing because there is no sunlight in here." I realised my oversight and complied.

I then explained the reason for my visit. When he heard what I had to say, he said, "That is a good idea! We can turn that into a sting operation." I didn't share his enthusiasm because it was against my conscience to compromise the ethics of my part-time occupation (which is, as you know by now, "investigative reporting"), and I didn't want to be labelled a Judas for any amount of silver, gold, dollars or whatever. Therefore I told him, "Sorry, oui, you'll have to find another actor to play the part of bait for your so-called sting." It must have dawned on him that I wouldn't budge on the stance I had taken so he said that he could not guarantee anything in that particular danger zone.

Left with little choice, I did my homework, and solicited information from a person who resided in the area. He briefed me on the various approaches to the "hole" (I did not tell him what I was about) and selected the route most utilised by clients, which had a somewhat steep descent that brings you directly into the centre of the hole.

When I mustered the courage and dared venture into this zone, forbidden to normal people, it had plenty characters hanging out around. I was swamped before I could ask any questions. The guys were quick on the draw. One guy said: "I have it! How much you want?" Another butted in, "My thing more proper" (bigger or more potent). Still another said: "I have the joints! Good weed, sensy!"

I asked, "Who tell all you I want anything?" One of them, a spokesman, made it his onus to answer. He said, "Once you come here is that you come for." I wanted to observe the whole scenario so I said, "Cool it, I not ready yet, is a partner I waiting for." Somebody replied, "Who is that? Mister doh coming. Check us out instead."

Trying to settle in, I asked one of them to buy a beer for me – a camouflage. I made sure I didn't give him more than five dollars. He tried nothing on me and returned promptly; then almost demanded, "Set me up now nuh, I want to buy a ten piece oui." I told him to hold the change and added a five dollars to his collection. He was so glad, he thanked me with a fist tag.

I observed the whole sequence from pusher to buyer. I found that the quantity to be rather small for a big ten dollars. It was a good thing I had on those shades which are like mirrors and make it difficult to know where one's eyes focus. The buyer didn't hide, but stayed right where he purchased his stuff and went through the process of hitting while I sipped my beer (I wanted it to last as long as possible).

Should I describe the hit? Well, he had his "tin" (a Fruta) close at hand. I noticed it had some small pin-like holes on the side (when in use horizontally, the holes are on the top side). He then presented from his pockets a matchbox of ashes from a used cigarette. He placed the ashes in the pin holes, then placed a piece of rock on top of the ashes, and lighted that combination while drawing on the normal can opening. I held my breath, I didn't want my system to become contaminated. In a twinkle of any eye (to me), that hit was over (it must have been a hit record).

But here is what freaked me out the most. I then saw the guy doing some strange antics. It appeared that he was seeing things I couldn't see, it also appeared that he was presently on a different plane of existence (PARANOID). He put his index finger across his lips, saying a silent "Sshh", and suddenly asked (his eyes searching all over the place), "Where them? They coming?" I strained my eyes and imagination but couldn't make head nor tail out of what he was saying. In ignorance I asked, "What you talking about? Nobody doh coming."

He pointed at what I would call imaginary beings and said convincingly, "You doh seeing those little men?" I didn't answer. I didn't want to make it obvious that I wasn't part of the crowd.

After a short while he seemed to settle into "his world" and then stooped down and started searching the ground repeatedly. I wondered what was going on. I thought that his contact lens had fallen out and he was searching for it, but I know that that was far-fetched. Another guy who was more in tune with these effects told him, "Parro, you too stupid, nothing doh fall, you smoke all already." He replied to the interferer, "Shut up before I come and look for you too!" That amused me.

Another thing I observed was that the attire of the majority of the personnel on that block was kind of dull. It appeared that they wanted to camouflage themselves or blend into their natural ghetto surroundings. Their main colours were black, brown, dark green, blue, gray, dirty white and the likes (I must have stood out conspicuously like a sore thumb with my bright, shocking colours).

After absorbing enough information, I wanted to quit but didn't quite know how to do it. One guy who maybe was getting uneasy about my presence asked, "Your partner not coming again man?" I replied, "I doh know nuh, but he tell me wait there for him."

I, too, was starting to feel uneasy and I wanted an excuse badly. Then the same person who had briefed me on the layout of the hole ran into me there. When he saw me there he was shocked. "Boy what you doing there?" he asked. "You brave pal! Them man should bwa kay you." That is, they should have robbed me!

In a cover up I said, "But you know, is you I waiting for so long. You messing me up man." And I made a signal with my hand, a downward motion for him to down play that scene, and used that opportunity to exit the drug hole. When I was leaving, a radical shouted, "Doh come back there! You hear?"

But I have no reason to go back anyway because mission was accomplished: result – successful. And the police? I doh meet not one nuh!

THE FRAME UP

I was about to enter my mother's residence when I heard the order, "Hey you, doh move!" I turned my head to see who gave the order. It was the police, drug squad to be precise. Although they were in plain clothes, I knew who they were because of one particular officer. I can clearly remember him telling me, "I have a plan for you." (It seemed somebody whom I had confided in sold me out and must have revealed who yours truly really was.) The cop had also said, "I know you good, you bound to be in it, you know too much!" But I wasn't afraid, I knew I was clean, as usual.

So I turned and raised my hands in mock surrender to the four officers. The cop who had the "plan" for me, said angrily, "I tell you 'doh move', you putting your hands up!" I was expecting a "normal" search, in and out, back and front but what followed took me completely off guard.

Boy, who tell you! I get one cuff! Straight in my right eye (instant black eye) I saw stars, and planets too! I heard a bystander say, "Is so nuh." "Shut up!" they ordered him, "before you get yours too". Man, in a twinkle of an eye, a massive crowd had gathered. It seemed long they hadn't seen some live action. But being no lamb, I put up some resistance, though I didn't go on the offensive.

Thinking it was a genuine "drug bust", and seeing the difficulty the "lawmen" were getting to subdue me, an eyewitness said unwittingly, "Is so they strong nuh when they smoke their thing." That made the officers more mad. Boy, look blows! Blows like old clothes. I thought that I was being run over by a Caterpillar. Trust me.

"What I do? I doh kill nobody," I asked. In answer, more blows. Who kick, kick; who jump on my chest, jump. My boy, I couldn't keep track the action was moving so fast and furious. Only a replay in slow motion could have given all the details, but nobody captured it on video.

Eventually, being outnumbered I was overwhelmed with police brutality. Put face down on the road, I was handcuffed with my hands behind my back (pure cinema) and hauled to my feet, my toes barely touching ground. Next, I was given a search as a formality. This produced a couple of joints that I had no previous knowledge of. (I can recall experimenting with that stuff decades ago but had now long passed that stage.) After, I was tossed into the back of a pickup like a rejected box of bananas.

I thought that that was the end of the VIP treatment, but I couldn't have been more wrong because when they took down me to the police station it was another instant replay. Other officers joined the party with no invitation from me and they were talking in strange tongues. It was "mother this" and "mother that". I thought only rude boys could curse but that is not true. You should have heard them in the police headquarters. After their fun and frolic, I was locked in a cold, damp cell with no facilities. I wasn't given bail, therefore I had to overnight.

An old classmate, we're from the same village, who had joined the force happened to notice me behind the bars. When he saw how my features were blown out of proportion (oversized lips, black eye, outstanding cheekbone, missing teeth, and abrasions (he even thought that I had a mango seed in one side of my mouth), he was forced to ask, "What happen? You was in a car-crash man, you should be in casualty paying your user fees and so forth." I explained the "scenes behind the scene", and he exclaimed, "Boy! what happen to them man, nuh!?" That question I really couldn't answer.

Next day I was brought to the magistrate's court early (While I was being transported there, you should see people trying their best to get a glimpse of me in the mobile "cage"). My turn came and I was asked to make a plea. I pleaded not guilty to the charge of possession of marijuana. I thought I could win because it was a frame up. Being broke, I couldn't afford to pay a legal advisor so I was left to fight my own battle.

Some say that lawyers are good liars, but they should have seen the combine police and prosecutor in action. They lie, they lie, they lie, they lie. Boy – look lies? Man they lied to the maximum! At one point they said that I was a "notorious" drug reporter who had been walking between the rain drops and not getting wet (obviously I must have had an umbrella – which is God) but that eventually I was caught red-handed. Can you imagine? Pure fabrication.

But then, whenever they told their "Nancy" stories, I noticed the presiding magistrate would glance at me with my innocent, and disfigured, look, to see if the stories matched the personality. My turn came to make my defence and I gave it my best shot. (I had no choice because despite those numerous spectators not one turned up as a witness.) My version of the story, coupled with my devastating appearance and "brutal" make-up, must have made an impact on the magistrate. But he just couldn't let me go scott free – it would have looked suspicious. So I stood in the box and awaited the dreaded verdict.

When I heard the magistrate say, "Guilty as charged, pay $5000 or three years' imprisonment," I fainted because I couldn't believe it. As I hit the cold floor, boop! I heard a distant voice saying in patois "Sakwe fenyan, ou pa ka leve!?" ("Damn lazy, you not waking up!?") It was my mother. And I realised I had just fallen from my bed! Oh boy, I was overjoyed to know that this distressing episode was, in fact, just another bad vision of the night. Thank you, Jah!

Man, I was so glad I had a hard drink first thing in the morning. Wouldn't you?

RUMBLE IN DE MARKET

The following is my latest release. And well, it's in the "exciting" class (The one you like! How do I know? It doesn't matter but I know though!). And well, it occurred in the market as in my title's allusion. Doh tell me you didn't hear about it! True, nuh!? I doh believe you, you lying! You maybe just want me to tell you again.

Notwithstanding, it was a Saturday morning. And I did not sleep the night before. You see, I was on a marathon run, partying round the clock. But when day broke on me, I thought that before hitting the carpet and taking a nap I would purchase one, or two, or more, jelly nuts in the market to rejuvenate my body and spirit a bit.

While going through the early-morning, bustling market square, glancing at the various country-fresh agricultural produce on display and being exchanged, I felt someone touching my pockets. I was alert enough to feel that, and, you know I don't like people touching me. So I turned and said (to whoever), "Yo! What you trying nuh?" And I saw it was a not-so-quick pickpocket, with my wallet in his hands, oui! And naturally, you should perceive that I was in a no nonsense mood! Therefore I instantly grabbed him in the collar, saying concurrently, "Before I kill your mother@$$, just give me my "Four-King" wallet!" (that's its brand name in case you didn't know).

He didn't comply and, instead, tried to abscond with it. So we wrestled a bit, and I successfully re-possessed my wallet. But in the scuffle he unwittingly broke my thick gold chain and it ended up in his hands. So thus I had managed to repossess my wallet but in the process he now possessed my most valuable, precious and treasured gold possession. (Persons usually link it to the underworld, i.e., drugs nuh, but I will give its true history. My girl bought it for me in St Maarten recently and she promised me solemnly if ever I should lose it, or come home without it, it is funeral home and cemetery for me!) So are you with me – in my instant plight?

In the slight pause that ensued, while I grappled rapidly with my dilemmatic thoughts, he must have sensed the sentimental sentiments or (death threat) emotions I had attached to it. Or he must have felt it a consolation token! Because he seized the opportunity of the lull in activity to attempt to get away – clean! I immediately gave chase. Boy! My life and peace of mind were at stake – and ran him down.

In my determination and desire not to concede loss, I bounced into, shoved, and pushed down vendors and buyers, ploughing into a number of stalls, and overturning tomatoes, cabbages, lettuce, and potatoes. I heard one irate vendor shout to me (in patois): "Patat manman" ("Your mother potato!"). But I wasn't interested in purchasing any for my mom (To tell the truth I didn't realise I had just unwittingly bought the whole lot of produce).

Reaching the outskirts of the market square, the guy started weaving in and out of the slow, crawling and sometimes standstill traffic along the river-bank road, going up to the bus terminals. And I found myself lagging behind. In desperation (no choice), I seized a bold initiative and without thinking (it seems I hardly do) jumped on the bonnet of a standstill but expensive SUV, and flew – or is it "fly" – in Superman goalkeeper fashion, and brought him down like a North American football tackle on the road surface. (Only in movies you does see that.) Reflecting, boy had I missed him, it would have been curtains for me. (My final act.)

First thing: I secured my gold chain, and commenced beating him with my fists (of fury) mercilessly. And you know nobody stopped me. They were just looking on. Luckily for him, the short arm of our law came on the scene; they were traffic ticket-issuing cops but played their part – arresting me. Then, you should hear the crowd of people: "Wicked! Mischievous!" etc. Me oui! They labelling so oui?! I countered, "All you doh see what he do me!?"

To add: the vehicle owner demanded a new bonnet, plus, a number of vendors came on the scene with a list of damage, and demanding compensation and so on. I had to consult a top-notch lawyer, who told me he couldn't help, but suggested I open a public assistance bank account, and hope some of my more ardent fans might bail me out. So if you miss me, you know what happen. I'll be chilling in the slammer.

AMBUSH
AFTER SCHOOL

Yes, they wanted to assassinate me! But before we venture into this earlier adventure, we must again utilise my personal laptop or desktop. No, you've got it wrong. It's not computer, but time machine, which, incidentally, only works in reverse (for the time being). And the time I have keyed in is back to school-time – just before I got expelled from primary school.

So brace yourself! I am about to activate the afore-mentioned time machine – and so – turn back the hands of time. Here goes. Zzziippp. Zap!

We reach oui! It was fast, eh? The date is now 19… But should I tell you, you might figure out how young I am? So we will leave it like that – you vex nuh?

And so, if my memory or time machine serves me well, in those days I was of a very humble and may say timid nature. And I would turn my cheeks endlessly (and tirelessly) for the oversized (and more stupid than me) school bullies to take advantage of. That was in the beginning – I have changed. But if you were my equal in size and age, it was a different story (both in the beginning-and-sometimes ending).

But what happened that specific "time" was at break time when I sought a little privacy and solitude and was about to feast my teeth into – and to savour – my mouth-watering, delicious recess. Up came this nuisance (from a blind spot) and, guess what? – downed my "delicacy". Boy! You mad! No hesitation, I turned from boy to beast, and like a raging Mike Tyson (or bull), I started dishing out kicks and cuffs like a wild

62

cat. And the untimely school bell saved him from going down (or under) as the teachers intervened like referees.

When asked for an explanation for my outburst, there was "no comment" from my quarter. I was insolent and seething with rage. If looks could kill – the nuisance would have been dead ten times over! Luckily, some other kids who had witnessed the cause of the fracas testified on my behalf and I was spared the rod or caning. And by the time school was over and being of a jovial disposition and unable to hold a grudge or injustice for any length of time, I soon laid that bout on the back burner.

And so, on my way home – as usual I strayed and made a "long cut", and found myself in the Botanical Gardens with some other peers. And when I left them and was approaching the northern gate, like a scene in a revenge and vengeance movie of the wild west, I found myself surrounded by four villains – that had one semblance. It is evident to me, today, that the biological genes of their respective DNAs were paternal; what I am trying to say is, I was being ambushed by a family of four brothers – for the incident I cited earlier. Three were older than me while the other, my equal in size and age, was the one I had had the bout with. To be honest, it was like an ambush in the night – as my day turned to night – as my little mind perceived their unholy intentions.

Having the comfort of his bigger brothers close at hand, my "enemy/friend" lunged into his attack with a jump kick. But being of an acute mind and reflex, I sidestepped, and as he went past executed a lock-neck hold: instinctively I realised I needed a "hostage" to bargain with. The three others closed in for the kill as I struggled to perfect my hold on my equal – and they contributed some blows to my person – and, unwittingly, to their blood brother as well – as I used him now and then to parry their blows, which, when I felt them, I would tighten my lock grip on my victim's neck. I thought for sure, I choking that one. (And I was determined to.)

As a further measure of defence "against the odds", I used my hostage (and shield) as a bargaining chip. "If all you hit me again – I breaking his neck!" I told them. Seeing that their little brother's eyes were bulging and his tongue was sticking out – and maybe turning blue, they backed off, but had their stones in hand to use, of course, once I had released my hostage.

Manoeuvring my hostage (against his will) closer to the Gardens' wall, I planned a desperate escape. When I saw that a loaded beverage distribution truck was coming down the Valley Road, I decided to utilise it in my daring getaway. As it neared, I suddenly freed my hostage, but not before giving him a final parting blow at the back of his head. He collapsed in a heap on the ground gasping for breath. Before the other brothers could gather their wits, I had scaled the wall and done a last-minute street crossing, in front of the "Coke is it" truck, frightening the driver, who applied his brakes and effectively screened yours truly from my enemies.

I made a running beeline through the Windsor Park to my home county – across the bridge and the Roseau river, not stopping for anything, event or person. But, do you know, up to this day I still see the brothers and, I believe, like me, they always remember that ancient scene, from my time machine.

THE LESSON

My latest project was not an assignment but rather a lesson. But you see me? I was an ardent karate student. My favourite martial arts' stars were Bruce Lee, Wang Yu, Chen Sing, David Chian, Jet Li. And so regularly I would go to karate classes, and I eventually moved up to the black belt grade. Along the way, I learned the various offensive and defensive routines and kicks: rotary, side thrusts, front kicks, back kicks and punches, blocks, karate chops and so on.

Naturally, I was very versed in the unarmed combat field. One of the more advanced lessons had to do with flying kicks, a Bruce Lee favourite. When my tutor started teaching that technique, I was very enthusiastic. I never missed these classes and I was the best pupil when it came to executing the flying side kicks. I practised it over and over again till I had it right. Once I tried it at home on my bed utilising the spring suspension of the bed. It gave me extra lift and flight but when I came down on the bed I broke a leg of the bedstead. My mother raised hell but being a sort of jack-of-all-trades, I was able to mend it with the help of some wood glue.

So, I really perfected that flying kick (to my mind). I even felt that I did it better than the teacher. He never accepted that though. He always said that I didn't quite have it right though he could not tell me where I needed improvement. But I was full of confidence executing that specific technique and was longing for an opportunity to use it. But it never turned up. When the troublesome fellas on my street knew I was an advanced karateka, they showed a lot of respect and said, "Boy, doh mess with mister, he know karate." So apart from the other students that I would spar with in free-style fighting (I couldn't intentionally make the blows make contact), there wasn't a genuine cause to utilise my favourite flying kick.

One Saturday afternoon, however, after walking my girl home in the Elmshall region and fantasising about winning the lotto, I was suddenly aware that a young man, a rough top, was approaching me from the opposite direction – it was just the two of us on that road. That didn't bother me but when I was about three yards away from him, he picked up a big stone (a poor man's gun) and confronted me menacingly and demanded, "Give me all the money you have on you now or else I bursting your head."

My boy, I got excited, my heart skipped a couple of beats – my chance had finally arrived. I thought that I could safely disarm him with a front rotary wiper kick. Hence, I asked, "You mad nuh?" Though I could have easily given him the money I had on me, I more wanted to use my skills than anything else.

I "shaped up", going into a pre-fighting stance. When the robber saw that, he realised that he had climbed the wrong tree and backed away looking for room to fire his missile at me. I rushed up to him, closing the gap quickly and disarmed him with a well-placed kick. When he attempted to pick up another piece of ammunition, I kicked him under his stomach, cramping him. While he lay on the ground recovering, I told him, "Stand up for more blows." He attempted to run away but I collared him and let him have a knee in his rib cage and a couple of karate chops and thumps.

As a last resort, he attempted a counter attack with a right-hand punch. I blocked it and punched him in his right eye. As he backed away, I gave him a side thrust kick in his chest, and he staggered backwards. I made one step forward, turned around and gave him a back rotary kick sweeping across his face. He fell flat on his back (using precision timing all my blows made proper contact), and only after some time did he manage to get shakily back on his feet.

I heard the guy apologising: "OK, OK. OK. Sorry, sorry, sir. I wouldn't do it again." And although I knew that he had had enough and had learnt his lesson...his lesson was – look before you leap...I still wanted to execute my favourite movement, the spectacular flying kick, live. So I jumped high into the air and turned on to my left side and executed a high-flying right side-kick. Maybe, I put in too much effort because I made extra height and I let him have it on the side of his head. But something must have gone wrong because I felt myself descending head first. Normally, I should have landed feet first. I felt a blow at the back of my head and suddenly had this strange feeling as if I was ten years old again: I could clearly recall a Christmas day in our drawing room with toys and presents under a tree with colourful lights.

I heard a faint voice that gradually got more distinct. It said, "Hey, hey, you know where you is nuh? " "Under the Christmas tree," I mumbled. I was seeing so many bright lights, like I was seeing the universe from a new perspective. I felt some cold water on my head. This revived me and when my sight cleared, a stranger was standing over me. I asked "What happen to me?" He said that he saw somebody running away as he arrived on the scene. I searched my pockets and found my wallet was gone.

It took a while for everything to fall back into place. It appeared that when I did that famous flying kick, I had knocked myself out cold giving my x-victim a golden opportunity to take my wallet. But he can call himself lucky strike if he got more than $10. As I had figured earlier, I could have easily given him the money because he maybe needed it more than me anyway.

I learned my lesson oui! Nowadays, I normally back down from fights. When people ridicule me, my excuse is usually, "I am a disciplined martial artist and I only fight as an extremely last resort." You would believe that? Few people do, so now go you and learn likewise.

GOING
UNDER COVER

I have plenty adventures under my belt but this episode is the "apex" – in terms of my audacity or just plain stupidity – beyond normal thought – reflecting: boy! I brave, oui!?

You know, in retrospect, I am yet to understand just how I allowed this politician guy to convince me to try a "Boy George" stunt! How that came about? Well, er, you see the politician approached me with this unsound proposal and assumption that I should and could easily infiltrate the hierarchy of the ruling party and obtain sensitive political information, like, if "they" plan to call an early or late snap election etc.

And like all my clients who look me up to do "odd jobs" for them, he told me that I was "good!" in fact "xtra good!" I felt flattered. But I had serious doubts in my mind (I didn't believe that I was that good an actor – or is it actress?) but my client was adamantly persuasive, offering a healthy monetary reward on the successful accomplishment of the assignment. Hence I became a major player embroiled in this cloak and dagger espionage scenario (for a few dollars more), and thus also was hatched this farfetched "plan" – this stunt. In a brief briefing, the opposition politician explained that the ministry of propaganda dissemination was most susceptible to the plan because its chief of staff was most fond of female company and was extremely talkative.

So let me disclose some details on how I went about it and then, how it went. First, I had to rehearse and practise my "graceful" moves. I didn't want to give off the impression of a "prostitute" – you check? I wanted total privacy so I implemented a James Bond strategy and rented an apartment on the outskirts, north of Roseau, that wasn't too heavily populated. Imagine – under my full feminine disguise, extra assets, etc I took a look in the mirror on the wall and nearly said, "Pssst", oui! That is to show just how "proper" I was. What you say? I nuts? I guess you're right.

But then, when D-(fatal) day arrived to put that crazy scheme into practical practice, I was nervous like hell. That's an understatement – if it was carnival it would not have been a major problem. I am sure you can understand the implication involved.

Well, before daring the streets, using my most practised effeminate voice, I called and made an appointment with the "top dog" of the targeted department, playing the perfect part of a curious female news reporter. And they fell for it (I fool them!). The next test: exiting my apartment. Before closing the front door, I noticed a questionable character idling about. So I turned around and using "double voice" tones carried on a conversation with myself in the house, playing like "this girl" had over-nighted with me, and went back inside, and turned on the TV – so the *voleur* would think that I was still inside long after I had left – as "she". I think it worked because when I returned (prematurely) nothing was amiss.

The third test was commuting on the bus. Well, one stopped, and it was packed like a sardine tin. The only seat I could obtain was between the driver and a third person. Boy look worries! Every time the man changing his gears, his hand on my knees. I gave him one no-nonsense look, and he realised that I would surely break his hand! So he apologised saying, "Sorry miss", and tried to make some conversation but I never responded – I was afraid my voice would croak or squeak or something of the sort – and sell me out.

After disembarking the bus in town, I paid the driver, and an inexplicable fear suddenly gripped me. I suspected that I was in for a "major" nervous breakdown. So straightway after disembarking I entered an adjacent shop licensed to sell liquors. And, using basic sign language. I ordered a "drink of rum" to tranquillise my nervous system. I heard a rum man say, "A moumou, nuh?" I flushed my drink and chased it with what I thought was water. Who tell you, it was more Soca rum, oui! I felt like fire was going down my throat. So I blurted out, "Water!" The same rum man said, "Aye, aye – the moumou can talk!" I quickly paid and left.

It was a very good thing I took that double drink, by accident, because as I was trying vigilantly not to faux pas on those tricky road surfaces with my high heels, I heard a "little voice" telling me, "Boy! You must be mad to really try that!" And I seconded the motion, and found myself saying, "Is true oui!" But the drinks stabilised me – somewhat.

But the biggest test was negotiating the Ministry steps in my high heels (I didn't practise that!). I tried my best using all my concentration, but midway up, my concentration broke when I tried to contemplate what would in fact transpire when I actually met my contact. That was – crucial, or was it a blessing in disguise? Because: I twisted my ankle, and forgot myself and hollered in my big Barry White tone of voice "Wee, Bon Dieu!

My foot break!" And the whole of the ministry sort of erupted, and began buzzing with mega excitement. Everybody was wondering, just who was that "nice" lady with that masculine voice? What would you do if you were in my shoes (high heels)? Doh lie.

Boy, to tell the truth, I felt like Cinderella in the ballroom when the clock struck midnight. I aborted the mission, ejected my high heels and descended the steps like an athlete doing hurdles. Man, I fled the government compound like a Dracula fleeing sunrise. Down Hillsborough Street I raced, onlookers were staring wide-eyed and wondering who was that crazy lady. Luckily for me I saw a friend's dark-glassed car held up in the traffic. I just opened his door and entered. The boy frighten. "My lady, what happen to you?! You crazy!?" he asked. When I "fly out" my wig and started to erase my make-up, realising it was me, he said: "Boy what happen to you – you mad nuh?" I answered, "I giving you anything you want – just bring me home right away. I'll explain later..."

Dumbfounded and spaced out he did. But hear that! Later, the politician asking me, "How it go?" I told him it was a disaster and I was lucky to get away with my brain, somewhat, still intact. He offered double the original amount if I should again attempt. But I told him straight, "Curse you and your money!" And you know, I can never ever try that again. What did you say? I getting progressively worse? I know oui, you don't have to tell me.

THE PRAYER MEETING

While trodding through a ghetto in the northern suburbs of Roseau one Saturday morning, on my way back from visiting my child's mother (I went to pay my dues – the price of a good time), I met this old acquaintance. We have known each other from way back when.

In our late, single-digit years, we used to play with our toy cars and trucks – voooommmm, voo-voom etc, mimicking engine-sound effects and screeching tyres. Then, in our early double-digit years, we rolled sèk (bicycle rims) and later in our early teens we played cowboy "me chance tee" (mischievous stuff), reminiscent of the wild and wicked west pwé kai (close to home). (Today it is a bit disorienting to note that our cowboy territory is now overgrown with houses and such schemes.)

We both attended the same primary and secondary schools. And in our late school years (the dread era), we experimented with the "erb". Since then, I moved on and out of that stage of the experiment, but my friend dropped out of school and settled down in that "stage" to become a sort of high priest in the ganga religion of Rastafarianism. It was like his holy herb was his religion and his religion was the herb. He got so caught up in this ganga occult that I nicknamed him "the most high".

Anyway, as I was saying, while passing through the ghetto in question, I met "the most high". He saluted me with all his Rastafari jargon: "Hail up, star! Jah! Rastafari! Selassie I..." etc, and went on to say, "Long Rasta (he) doh sight de I (me)." I responded (as much as I could) identical to him: "I and I (me) just there man" and went on to say, "I man, just come from paying my maintenance fees and blah, blah, blah, etc" just letting my mouth idle.

While conversing loosely, he mentioned that he was on his way to an informal prayer meeting and that they were going to bless their new church. Being a Saturday and having nothing extra essential to do, and knowing as well that the venue he referred to was in my county, I thought that I would go along just to kill time.

When we came to the site of – what I must call – an unorthodox church, I was mildly taken aback. I should have expected that. It wasn't a strong building just an old wooden shack, a one-room house. And there we met two other members of his church – characters with extra long natty dreadlocks, which served as testimony to their long-rendered membership of this mystic sect. They greeted each other with great fanfare, ado and what-have-you expounding on the creator's various names and titles, while mildly acknowledging my "baldheaded" presence. They tried unsuccessfully to convince me to "switch on" (put on) my dreadlocks as a sign of respect and reverence to the creator and the black king from the east (Hail Selassie). The battle was hot – three to one, but I adamantly maintained "to each his own order".

Anyway, the time came for them to go through their strange religious ritual, and for me to experience this weird, mind-freaking out phenomenon. First thing, after entering the church shack, respect had to be shown to the (real) most high God and for the holy weed by removing all headgear and wear and by shaking their big and long bongo, congo, natty dreadlocks. Naturally, being a baldhead (so to speak) I had nothing to shake, but I was allowed observer status.

Next, the holy weed was brought out in a calabash. I estimated the amount to be a pound – let me tell you, a pound is plenty weed. Then the "cha la wa" (chalice or peace pipe) was also brought out (I was taking mental notes) and filled to the brim, then came the fireworks (matches) and, boy, chalice started to blaze! While they chanted and sang Jah praises, one said, "Pass de chalice on the left-hand side and let it burn! And let all the wicked run. Jah Rastafari." A little later, the second accomplice offered me the peace pipe, saying, "Lick the chalice, and let it blaze and change your dirty ways." "Just cool," I responded, "I-man safe!" and allowed the chalice to bypass the I (me).

Boy, look smoke! I saw smoke bellowing from their nostrils like two mufflers or, more like, fiery dragons from stories of ancient Persian tales and myths. The smoke of the burning weed filled the atmosphere of the church shack – they "smoked" me, like smoke meat. After sometime I started feeling light-headed and "too dee" (dizzy). Or was it a high? (because I have forgotten what it feels like).

At the heights of the session, I heard a siren in the distance. It sounded like an ambulance, fire engine or police siren. That concerned me but the cops were not known to frequent that neighbourhood (often). The sound got louder . So I told the sect members, "Fire in the area man?!" They were unperturbed, unconcerned and very complacent, and continued to indulge in their ganga ritual. One remarked, almost casually, "Babylon have fe burn, star," and took a couple big draws on the chalice, then choked, and stalled and commenced backfiring – coughing uncontrollably – with tears streaming down his face, beard and down to his garments.

The "most high" retorted, "Oh, how very good and pleasant it is for brethren to dwell in peace and unity! It is like the precious ointment upon the head, that ran down upon the beard, on the beard of Aaron etc" (Psalm 133). The siren continued to wail loudly while the smoke of Jah weed filled the so-called temple. But hearing some commotion and excited voices talking outside, I got curious and wanted to see where the fire was located. I also wanted some clean fresh air so I asked permission to open the sole side window on the street side of the shack. They just shrugged their shoulders and refilled their "cha la wa". But like all typical Dominicans, I wanted to know first hand what was going on out there. Therefore I unlatched the window and peered outside while some smoke also took that opportunity to escape and dissipate.

Boy! Without warning, the firefighters outside suddenly and simultaneously open fire on the shack with their water cannons. The unexpected impact sent me backwards, crashing into the far partition, scaring the living daylights out of the members of that dread cult! My long-time friend, the "most high", said, "What de mother @$$!" Another exclaimed, "Holy Smoke!" The other, "Oh Jah, another flood."

My friend, I guess you know what had transpired. A neighbour, meaning well and thinking "Where there is smoke there is fire" called the fire brigade. And they came and did the rest, that is, destroyed the shack with their overpowered appliances.

And that was the end of the prayer meeting...yes oui. Amen.

FOUR O'CLOCK ROAD BLOCK

Yo. You see me? I do not believe in putting all my eggs and breakables in one basket. Hence I tend to spread it around. So I do not believe that my writing skills (alone) will see me through this life without hitches, thus I have become and consider myself as an all-rounder. So being well diversified, I went into the countryside to do a session of hard work and to come back down with something of value as well – remember the good Lord said by the sweat of your brow and body you will eat bread etc.

Well, that day the sun was extremely hot, and I sweated a lot. (I thought that at the end of the day – for all my sweat – I would eat a bakery of bread.) Now, why I worked so hard is because I didn't want Satan to employ my idle hands. So after I had toiled and tilled the land that my body evolved from and must return to, I felt good that I had done something positive and productive.

But before returning to city life, I collected an over-sized bag of "weed" and walked down from my garden to the junction where our feeder road met the main road, to "ketch" a ride to town. I didn't mind walking with the bag of "weed" on my head (all that is part of my day's work) but when the junction came in view, an unfamiliar sight met my eyes, it was a four o'clock police road block! I paused to assess what was happening (I was about 25 yards or so away). And out of the bush, on the left-hand side of the road, emerged a policeman in his army combat fatigues, machine-gun in hand. If he hadn't spoken, I would not have seen him. He introduced and identified himself as a police officer. "So long I know that!!" I said.

He went on to say that they were conducting a search for drugs. "You in the wrong place at the wrong time," I told him. "Try the pharmacy in Roseau."

"You playing smart, eh?" he replied. "OK narcotics!!"

"What is that?" I asked, like it was the first time I heard that word.

"Marijuana," he said, breaking the word down.

"I doh know nothing about that," I said.

"We are also looking for illegal firearms," he continued, unconcerned about my response. "I do not belong to any paramilitary organisation," I told him. "I am unarmed and un-dangerous. My only arms is my two arms."

"What you have in that bag Mr Smart?" he then inquired. I revealed the plain truth: "grass!" I saw his face change, for the better. I could also see the gleam in his eyes. I reckoned he saw the real possibility of promotion in the ranks of the drug squad.

"What was its street value?" he inquired.

"I doh know. I never sell grass before," I replied, and wondered why was he interested in that aspect.

He retorted, "Play smart still!!" And with a cocky nod, he called on his comardies lower down the road, saying, "OK, we can call it a day! Look, I hold a pardner there red-handed with a bag of weed. It may be have a street value of two million."

"If that is true, why are we wasting time cultivating bananas?" I thought. I could buy ten pick-ups.

The rest of the drug patrol ran over like excited school boys, a couple of them started "touching up" the bag. They commanded, "All right, come with us. Board the van!"

I said coolly, like the ice man, "No problem..."

One responded, "If everybody we hold was like you, eh, life would be a dream."

"You better wake up!!" I said in my mind.

As I boarded their van, I asked casually, "So what all you going and do with all that grass?"

"After we get you convicted, we will burn it together with other drugs at Morne Bruce," the officer in charge replied.

"All you well brave, you mean (that I hear) all you going to burn all those drugs without protective masks?" I went on, "The amount of smoke all you will inhale in one session is more than a parro head will smoke in his whole lifespan. Some of all maybe parro and doh know. No wonder they say all you in it!!"

They did not like what I said. But one purporting to understand what I was implying, commented, "Ooohh, that maybe is why I like to go on these drug missions." But before driving off they put handcuffs on me. "There is no reason for that. I well wanted a ride to town, anyway," I told them. They didn't worry and just said, "When we reach headquarters we will take it out, just behave yourself before we fatten you!"

Well yes, the ride came at the right time. I even said God sent it. But passing through the various villages en route to the capital, I could hear the meditations of curious onlookers. "They hold that one!" was their unanimous thoughts.

Arriving in the city, they brought me into the gates of

Babylon HQ. Some officers who were "ketching" their legal alcoholic high in the canteen came over to see the latest catch. And to clout me. But strange enough, none seemed to be bothered to verify the evidence. It must have been an oversight.

They took me to the second floor of the main building, making a right turn at the top of the stairs, and we entered the drug squad section, where they straightaway commenced interrogating me from all angles. One laid out a map of the island and asked me to pinpoint the location of the marijuana plantation.

When I heard that, I put on a big act, making as if my night had suddenly turned to day! I said, "Soooo, that all you was thinking of nuh??! All you mad man! I doh know nothing about marijuana plantation!"

The inspector , who wasn't at the road block but now on hand, asked, "So what do you have in the bag?" Again I stated, "Grass."

As if to re-emphasise the way they originally thought, he said, "Well?!?..."

"So?" I said in a defiant tone. And a little after, "So, what?!?..."

He realised something was wrong somewhere, so he told one of his men, "Open the bag." And there it was, the "green grass of my country home", as I had earlier admitted.

"What kind of grass is that?" asked the officer who had opened the bag in bewilderment . He freak out.

"Grass for my rabbits!" I confessed. So you see, I am indeed well diversified – I even rear rabbits.

The officers who had caught me "green" handed, suddenly got disillusioned. They realised that their hopes for fame, recognition and promotions were dashed. They were angry to the bone, and started mutating. I sensed they were tempted to teach me a serious lesson that I wouldn't forget in a hurry. I panicked. But the inspector would have none of that. Praise God. Instead, he gave them a tongue lashing, exposing and expounding on their stupidity and greed for promotion (right in front of me).

"Go at your home boy," he told me without further ado. And turning to his officers, he gave them a stern warning. "When all you see mister on the road, doh trouble him!" As I was leaving with my legal grass, I gave the lawmen a taunt, saying softly, "BEEAA, all you cannot touch me doh?!"

And so far I have been living happily ever after! Thanks to the inspector! Yes oui.

"GUADA" CONNECTION

After the report of my "close shave" in Montego Bay, I was contacted by a leading newspaper editor, who told me: "I want you to investigate the 'back-door connection' between Dominica and Guadeloupe."

I was so taken aback, I said to him, "You bound to be joking! I nearly get five years' jail for my fastness in Montego Bay. What you trying, nuh?" Anyway after enough argument he managed to convince me that I should give it a try.

Well, to start from scratch I wanted to do it right and safe, therefore, I went to the French consulate for a visa. I wanted to be "legal". But then I learned that I had to go all the way to St Lucia for a visa. So I was left with no alternative but to go the real illegal way. I found a partner, a drug trafficker, who was a veteran in the "back door" runnings. He assured me that he had a safe and reliable "captain" to traffic us across the channel.

So we made our preparations. We hired a transport and late after sundown went down the west coast to a certain village where he purchased some "weights" of cured top-class weed (sency). I pleaded to my new-found friend that I didn't want to "fall" and take jail in Guadeloupe. He told me, "Relax, I know what I doing." I replied, "Ooohhh Kay pal" being not too convinced.

We then went farther down, past Portsmouth, making a detour around the police station to the "Gulf" where our captain was waiting with a few other passengers. (I found the trafficking of passengers to be a very lucrative venture. We paid the captain well over $500.) We were seven passengers in all. I found comfort in the number 7. I thought it to be a lucky number.

We began our journey on the waters close to midnight. I was filled with apprehension. I didn't know what to expect, we were travelling in pitch-black darkness – it was a moonless night. After beating "waters" for sometime, the engines suddenly cut off. I said, "Damn, doh tell me we have engine trouble already." I didn't fancy the idea of drifting on the high seas – Jaws also came to mind. The captain said, "Sshhh. Everybody quiet!"

It was then I heard the low drone of an engine but I couldn't see anything. It took a while before I could recognise a big black shape passing across the bow of our rather small fishing boat. It was apparently the coast guard (with no navigation lights) looking for people like us. I realised that the captain "did know his onions". Not long after we restarted our engine and continued our travels.

But when we reach the real channel, boy! Look big waves! Man! I saw waves big like the ministerial building. Serious. I was "kapon!" (scared to my wits' end), but I noticed that my fellow travellers were quite calm. I asked my partner if the channel was always so. He answered, "Usually". I started praying silently. (Today I am still convinced that it was my prayers that saw us through.)

After x amount of hours we passed the Saints and I noticed other lights ahead. My partner confirmed to me "that is Guadeloupe". So we got our stuff together. Both our clothes and goods were wrapped in plastic bags to prevent them from getting wet because my friend had forewarned me that we might have to "swim for it" (In retrospect I have reached this conclusion that all who ply these waters regularly or often in this mode of transportation are indeed living dangerously).

While we were still a far distance from land, it looked like a mile to me (I am not that good at estimating distances), the captain ordered: "Jump overboard!" I refused. Point blank, I said "No way! You must be mad! I am not going and make no headlines tomorrow, for them to say 'man's body was fished out of Guadeloupe's waters!'" The captain retorted, "You want them French men to seize my *@!?*% boat, man," but I remained adamant.

Reluctantly he went closer, then asked if it was OK for me. While I was trying to make up my mind, saying "Well, let me see…" he suddenly pushed me overboard "ju-joom!" together with my belongings. I now had no choice! Well, the swim to shore was uneventful, but I was longing for my feet to touch dry land.

Eventually it did. We dressed and immediately made for higher ground. When we reached the road and I saw the width of it, it was like wow! "Alice in wonderland". I was so freaked out that I nearly got spotted by the first vehicle that appeared. My partner shouted: "Duck! doh let the headlights flash on you!" I dived into a bush by the roadside just in the nick of time.

My accomplice explained that if the gendarmes saw anybody walking that particular area at this time of night, they were sure to get picked up. So we were extremely careful as we made our way to a bus stop, where we took a bus to the capital, Pointe à Pitre.

When the extent of progress and development going on registered in my head, I felt like a true country boy. I noted that Dominica and Guadeloupe were comparable to chalk and cheese when it came to "movements". I often used to wonder what it was in "De Guada" that dazzled our youths. So, now I know.

But my first appearance on the famous Shemin Feur (Iron Street – so named because of the old railroad iron tracks laid there) was quite dramatic. I saw fellas scattering all over the place. I asked my tour guide what had happened. He laughed and explained that it was a case of mistaken identity. He said that I had an uncanny resemblance to a feared notorious French police officer popularly known as "Fly". When the "Radicals" recovered their wits, things returned to normal.

I saw all sorts of bad elements buying and selling drugs. I put on my "baddest" attitude; I remembered the saying, "When in Rome do as the Romans do." I witnessed drugs selling like hot bread (yes oui!). I said no wonder them drug lords are so "big up" or wealthy back in DA. I met a "youtman" that I knew well back home; we greeted each other with a knuckle tag. He then proceeded to give me a run down on his recent activities in Guadeloupe. He confessed among other bad deeds that he especially enjoyed "bwa kaying" (robbing) French people, saying how he would "tear gas them" and grab their gold chains – and run! He gave me invaluable information. I sympathised with him and said, "I can understand the scene man. You is a mad fella, but the way

Dominica is, if I was younger I would be just like you." (Most probably?)

But hear that! Around two days later, while I was there just chilling on the block, taking in the scene, a ride just pulled up. I do not know what transpired because I don't understand the French language fluently, but I just saw "them man" pull out guns and start to exchange hot lead in the ghetto! Believe it or not I was caught in a crossfire. You believe it is a joke! I don't know how I did it, but miraculously I got away without a shot!

When the actions subsided, I said to myself, "That is it! My boy, enough is enough." I had got more than I bargained for. My partner told me that he was going back by boat. I said shaking my head, "Ah Ah, Ahh, wa, not me!"

How did I return? Tricks of the trade my friend. I gave myself up to the French immigration authorities. I told them "straight" that I was an illegal alien who wanted to be deported. They tried their best to interrogate me but to no avail. I couldn't understand what they were saying and vice versa. So they put me on a plane to Canefield. It took just 25 minutes and I was back home – safe and sound.

JAIL BAIT

It was Carnival Tuesday afternoon and I was a spectator standing with a rum and Coke in one hand, on a corner in downtown Roseau, watching the revellers going by. You see, I am not the guy who likes publicity. So I was waiting for after dark to take to the streets (last lap) and I do not have that much stamina to last many rounds anyway.

And while watching the more bold ones and those that were more drunk go by, I recognised a young school number that used to give me "good vibes". However, she appeared to be under the age of consent. Jail bait. Therefore, I used to keep my distance (I later learnt that she was of the age). But here I was seeing her scantily dressed, in wicked pom-pom shorts that left very little for my extra-creative imagination. That made my blood boil and, worse, she was moving like a worm in the band (wining and rolling). That got me excited. Plus, she made an invitational sign with her big brown eyes that sent my pulse-rate racing. Naturally, Adam being my forefather, I was being led into temptation headlong.

I flushed the remainder of my drink, threw away the plastic glass and made an "inter-rolling sign" with my hands (meaning that I would like to check her later). I also said some unspoken words; she had to read my lips. They were, "You'll see when I hold you tonight." (You see, my main girl was in the foreign for vacation and I didn't mind a temporary replacement. And these days of revelling offered the rare opportunity to do a number of crimes safely. Not true?)

As the unofficial time for the rendezvous approached, I started to take a couple of "steps-ups" (wine and rum mixed). These were like turbo-chargers for my drink high. But I was careful not to cross the dead-drunk line before I would be too drunk to recognise my potential target.

She was the type that could make a lot of angels think twice about keeping their positions in heaven. Being a weaker vessel, my resistance was melting down. Not wanting to wait for the last minute and maybe lose that chance, the next time I came across her I called her over. The drinks had made me lose all inhibitions and I grabbed her around the waist and we joined the band.

Not being a "ruff neck" we took it in the easy section, chipping at the back of the big truck. (It was not sundown yet.) I noticed a number of envious eyes from both sexes, but then I was feeling good. She asked me, "What you was waiting for nuh? Long I ready for you oui." But I still had second and third thoughts. With all my drunkenness, I was aware that what I was holding on to was a possible 14 years in jail (if anything should materialise). So I tried to exercise as much self-control as possible.

But when the sun went down and it became dark, I changed my position and collided with her back bumper. We were no longer two individual entities but were now united as one. Girl, I stuck on her like crazy glue! Turning her head round she told me, "I can feel you." I just nodded in acknowledgement and we just kept moving like a trailer truck, she was the truck and I was the trailer. I was following the leader (now, do not think I've joined the porn club) and that sequence of things caused me to understand why the first man was so easily led into sin by the woman God gave him. (You follow??)

We made about four rounds on the carnival route and I wondered if I could repeat a similar feat later? The end of the jump up came as an anti-climax to me. I wished it could have gone on a little longer, I was feeling so nice.

She told me that she had to go to school the next day so I decided to walk her home, which was a considerable distance. Walking with her didn't raise much eyebrows as it would have done under normal circumstances. Along the way there was a number of isolated places where I could have ravished this (almost) willing victim. I was feeling that she wanted to be abused but knowing the pressure I would get from Joe public, I strongly resisted the temptation (my resistors were glowing red hot).

We reached the base of the Fond Cole hill, and I asked her where she lived. When I saw the mountainous region, I exclaimed, "Right up there!" But I agreed to do the full honours of an escort but warned her, "I hope you doh have a boyfriend around there that would want to burst my head with a big stone." She told me, "Fear no more" (I wondered if I still could trust that political slogan).

We reached the house where she resided with her mother (her father didn't claim responsibility for her) with no incident, but I was totally exhausted (the hill was a work out). She introduced me to her mother who was still awake and from all indications appeared to be a veteran reveller. She had this fiery, dragon-like alcoholic breath (the second-hand fumes revitalised my "high"). "You looking like a nice gentleman," she told me (looks are really deceiving). "I like you for her, take good care of my little baby eh. If you can buy schoolbooks and uniform for her that would be very nice of you. "

"What? The mother selling the girl for me man?" I said in my mind.

And after talking a bit and putting on a nice performance, it was time for me to go. It was almost midnight, but the mother recommended that I overnight. I declined the hospitality, but the mother was adamantly persuasive so I gave in to her strange demand. I said to her I would sleep on the couch in the drawing room. But the mother would not let me. She said it was all right for me to sleep in her daughter's room with her.

My heart skipped a couple beats when my mind registered what was being said so I went into the room where the girl was already sleeping (it appeared).

Then, I heard the mother say "but for safety..." I thought she was going to hand me a "protection", but, she continued "... I will put two pillows to separate all you on the bed." That she did. So I laid down on "my side" of the bed (like a cowboy, only removing my sneakers) and prayed to God, "Lead me not into this temptation". And he heard my prayers (although today when I revisit that sequence of events I wish he hadn't answered my prayers). After staying awake while my conscience battled temptation, I fell asleep, to be awakened at dawn by the cock crowing in the neighbours' yard.

The girl took a bath and her mother made me some coffee.

It went down well although I hoped it didn't contain a "stay home dumpling" formula – a love potion that results in instant marriage. When the girl was ready for school, I bade her mother farewell and walked the girl down to the bus stop.

While walking, I told her to take her schooling seriously – a fatherly talk, nuh? Then, a sudden gust of wind took her $40 NBA (Bulls) cap and floated it over a six foot galvanize fence. Immediately, I started to climb the fence to retrieve it. Halfway over, she commanded, "Leave it alone! Come down!" I paused and asked if there was a big bad dog in the person's yard, and wondered maybe I was being an idiot and could have used the gate entrance instead. She reiterated, "Come down I tell you!" So I did. Baffled, I asked her to explain herself. So she explained: "Last night you couldn't jump two pillows, but look now you want to jump a six-foot fence for an old cap!"

My boy! Not another word I could utter…

AFTER MIDNIGHT

One day, in the middle of the night, I had this awareness of something strange going on or about to happen. It is a weird phenomenon that is hard to fully explain, and I am not too sure if I was awake or asleep and dreaming that I was awake – and experiencing that scene. I looked out of my bedroom window into the dark night and saw a (to my mind) suspicious-looking person, dressed in jet black with a big black coat (Or was it a cloak? Or it might have been a cape!) and a black hat like a shadow standing under the lamp post a little higher up our street

It appeared that he had an appointment or a rendezvous with somebody or something. Naturally, my mind came on a potential "night shift" worker, a ninja robber. But he seemed a rather confident one (if he was one) – and it also appeared he had all the time in the world to waste away. But what struck me as extra odd was when I saw two police officers on their night beat walk past the black figure standing eerily in the shadow of the lamp post as if nobody was there. I thought: these two officers certainly do not share my suspicions (or was it possible they hadn't seen him at all?).

I really do not know why I did the following, because though I like to fantasise about playing "detective", I usually leave that to pen and paper. But then I saw the mystery man take a look at his watch and then up the street, and then commence to walk casually up in that direction.

Curiosity can really kill anything. I got out of bed, flashed on a shirt and a pair of soft shoes (I do not don pyjamas except for special occasions, like hospital etc) and followed my suspect like an agent, ducking here and there. When he arrived in a certain residential area he seemed to be lurking around, looking for a potential place of entry. In an effort to thwart a robbery attempt, I shouted to the man in black, who was about five yards away in the darkness, a sharp, "Hey! I see you!" Now it was more as a alarm to scare him away. But it didn't work because the guy just turned like a real cool customer and said, "Oh, so you have been observing me." He continued, "How comes you see me, people usually doesn't see me when I am on my 'runnings'. They does only see the effects when I done."

I panicked – my mind told me, "You see what you look for!" Thinking he was going to attack me, I quickly engaged the "get set" mode and prepared to take flight. But it just as quickly registered that he was not the violent type so I aborted my cowardly thought, and, instead, I asked, "Wha, what you doing there??"

He replied in a toneless tone, "I working."

"At this time of night!?" I queried.

"But how?" he replied, apparently not seeing the logic of my inquisitve concern. "I am on my tour of duty", he continued. "I work at anytime for my master".

Master? We usually call our employers boss, bigger boss and boss man,"big man", "papa", "godfather" (in the drug underworld) and so on. But master? That sounded strange and foreign to my ears. I speculated: if he is not what I originally thought he was, then he most probably is one of those crazy, lunatic and mad personnel who does from time to time come from wherever and just pop up on the local scene. So to "stretch it", I asked, "Just who is that grand master, pal??"

"You right," he replied, in full control. "He is a grand master, but plenty of his people that owe him doesn't pay their due respect to him. That is why he does send me anytime, sometimes without a notice to "collect".

I felt he was holding something back so I inquired, "To collect what?"

"You doh find you too inquisitive?!" he retorted. I shrugged my shoulders in reluctant agreement. But he continued. "I'll tell you... a lot of people doh like my boss man although he does treat them proper. Some of them mistreat his messengers and does disrespect my boss when he trying to put them straight and to make them fall in line. So, as the most steadfast and loyal employee of the bigger boss, I does have to carry out the dirty work so to speak, and I do carry it out to the letter. You cannot buy me nor bribe me – and for that I am hated."

I started to suspect drug links, but the area he was monitoring was not drug infested, and I should know because I live there. That added to my confusion, and, as if he was sensing that, he said, "I going and tell you something that will freak you out even more..." I said to myself, "The guy is a psychic."

"Me and my boss," he revealed, "is one, though some are of the opinion that he is 'good' and I am 'bad', while some see it vice versa. But between us we complement each other – one cannot exist without the other. It is like if there is no beginning then there is no end and vice versa. My boss," he continued, "is considered to be omnipresent – infinitely at large. I too! You see I can carry out my work in several places at the same time."

My thoughts reverted to now I know he really mad for true because I doubted he was referring to a web site on the internet. To reconfirm and hoping to assess the scenario in full, I asked, "So all now so, you working??"

"That I telling you," he answered.

I queried, "You serious?? ... Your head working good?"

In answer, he asked me a two-part question. "What happen? You blind and cannot hear?"

"I feel you mad..."I responded, and concluded, "You bound to be mad." Just as I said so the midnight church bells began ringing in the distance.

"That's your opinion," he replied, "but I going. The right time come for me to deliver and to collect."

He departed, walking briskly and with a sense of purpose. I watched him disappearing into the darkness, and as if sensing my eyes piercing into his back, he turned and said, "Expect a visit from me... any time in the future..."

I replied, "Shut your face!!" and with that he faded out.

While still gazing in his direction, I saw two police officers emerge from the darkness. They were (apparently) the same two I saw earlier.

When they were close to me, I asked: "All you doh see a partner in black going up the street?"

"No," they answered. I couldn't believe it. "But now there!" I emphasised, "I was talking to the man."

The cops watched me suspiciously, then each other, and

said to me, "We want to search you!" They found nothing of (their) interest on me, so I returned home and sat on my bed wondering about the preceding events before dropping off into another journey into dreamland.

Well, the break of day greeted me on my bed wondering what the visions of the night meant. But I have no experience in the field of dream interpretation and I was uncertain as to what really transpired Was it a dream, semi-dream or reality? But I was disoriented when one of the residents in our street broke the early morning news to my mother that somebody had died in our street.

Well is now I freaked out. My mind started to touch base with a lot of possibilities. Could the "mystery man" have been a killer or hit man? You maybe saying I watching too much TV. Would I have to endure a gruelling session of interrogation at the hands of the CID because I had a close encounter of the weird kind with a probable killer? I started getting nervous and anxious because two police officers had seen me out on the streets last night.

I wondered who was the victim, and heard the news carrier call the dead woman's name. It was around her area that the "prowler" had been lurking.

Now curiosity killed me dead. I got up from my bed and went into the drawing room where my mother and friend were discussing the latest "radio mouth" news broadcast "Weh, weh, weh, when she die nuh?" I stuttered.

"After midnight."

You should know what was going through my brain, so I asked: "How, how, how she die nuh?"

My mother's friend answered, "Bassil that kill her..."

"Bassil!?" I retorted, and asked myself, Who the F was Bassil? Was Bassil the name of my murder suspect? Seeing the bewildered look on my face, my mother's friend eased the strain on my mind and put my wits and meditation back in place and order saying, "She died of cancer."

"Oh I see," I said because my night had turned to day. I then remembered that in local parlance Bassil is the name of the mythical messenger of death. And the deceased had been diagnosed with cancer of the first degree (whatever that meant) so we could have expected the worst.

But that still left me deep in wonderland territory. Was my midnight experience really real? Did I speak with death? Or vice versa? I remembered the words of the creator's son about his second coming like a thief in the night. And the other aspect of his promise: "I'll be back... for you", meaning you and me. That was weird, wasn't it?

The next thing: the boys on our block have it saying that I getting mad because somebody heard me talking to myself big night, oui!

LIVING DANGEROUSLY

Many persons are not aware that Guadeloupe is like a training ground for those who would like to make crime their career. In other words, it is a gangster's paradise. Perhaps it's because of the French people's attitude where they take it that the dead victim is the one in the wrong. And the next incentive is – their jail nice! Ask those who have experience of it. Therefore, outlaws don't think twice about pulling the trigger. And do you know some of those people are actually walking around and going to and fro between Dominica and our French sister islands?

Let me share a (realistic) experience. Are you ready to take the ride with me? OK. Jump in and let's have some fun (if you think it's fun).

One of my more dangerous episodes happened in the "Guada", aka Guadeloupe, during one of my early escapades there. I was still green and didn't yet have the feel of the ropes so I enlisted in a gang of four-seasoned gangsters based in Point-a-Pitre. But I always carried with me as an amulet – a secret weapon – my Bible (a mini pocket-size version). My colleagues thought it incompatible with our occupation but, between you and me, it is what rescued me from the path I was on.

One night, the gang, including me, decided to make a daring late-night robbery at an out-of-town gas station. I wasn't in too much favour of the idea but I know that I was running away from tribulation back home in Dominica or, maybe, I was also running away from myself (my conscience). But I warned or pleaded with them, "Not to shoot nobody." The leader said, "It's OK man, we shoot enough people already." I raised my eyebrows but I was learning the hard way – by experience. It gives the exam together with the lesson.

Before setting off on this wrongly motivated mission the veterans said that they were going to "bad up" their heads. I figured that was to bolster up their courage. I, not being a partaker of that specific illegal substance on their agenda, settled for a dose of alcohol to tranquillise my nervous system, and I had quite a few, I must say. And after, we cruised on down the highway.

We pulled up – in our stolen ride – a distance away from the service station on our hit list, to monitor personnel and customers on hand. As it got closer to the midnight hour, motorists became sporadic. The gang leader eyed his watch and said, with a deep breath, that the time was now and now was the time. I repeated my concerns about "gun play". The leader said that that would be unnecessary and that the job would be a piece of cake but if I felt uneasy I could always back out. I should have, but it was a considerable distance to walk back at that time of night, so I stayed on and prayed that it would work favourably. That prayer, I know, was ill-conceived.

Anyway, we pulled up alongside the refilling station and an attendant in his mid-twenties came over to service our vehicle. We got out and I told him, "Reach for the sky!" He did not respond and seemed confused so I said, "Hands up!" He still did not do as ordered. But I soon realised my amateurish mistake when my colleagues gave "like" orders in French while brandishing their hand wear. They dragged him back to his cash register while I kept a nervous look out. Hearing some commotion and angry talking in the office, I, being impatient, went over to check it out. The leader of the gang, it seemed, was not pleased with the night's taking. It quickly became frighteningly evident that something deadly was imminent.

Boy, as I uttered, "Boy! No boy!"...Too late! I heard blam! blam! in quick succession and blam! again and saw it – live. A slaying in – what I must confess was – "stupid blood". I saw the guy fall in a pool of blood.

Dumbfounded, almost speechless, I asked, "But, but why?" The leader gave me an indifferent look and asked apathetically, "You want to take his place?" I tend not to show my true emotions (that is how I is) but it touched my innermost being. It was a mixed feeling – sadness and remorse. But I had little time to brood or mourn over the victim because we all heard a police siren in the distance. We jumped into our getaway vehicle and while attempting to put some distance between our respective vehicles (the outlaws and the law), one of the veteran accomplices asked the trigger man the same question. "But why you shoot him?" The leader and driver replied almost casually, "I just wanted to try out my new gun, man, and he is a damn donkey not to have more money anyway."

Suddenly, there was a bright light lighting up our world and vehicle – it was a searchlight. I looked out and up and it was almost like the sun was out (I mean, on!). My boy, gendarmes in helicopter, like a scene out of a blockbuster movie. I regretted all the events of the night – even to my birth.

As we rounded a tight corner, up ahead was an effective police roadblock. Instinctively the driver and gang leader turned off the road and into a cane field. Ahead of the vehicle, I saw the cane plants parting company and making way like a ship in water. And, suddenly, there was this big stone in our path, and "de-gan!" we jam it. The sudden halt caused me, occupying the other front seat, to head-butt the windscreen, smashing it. With all that, I was out of the vehicle in a flash and beside the leader dashing through the cane field like madmen trying desperately to distance ourselves from the abandoned vehicle.

Not too far from the scene, I heard the excited voices of the French police as they caught up and discovered our last piece of evidence. Then the hunt was on. I was trying my utmost to keep abreast of my leader in crime but running in the canefield was something else, and at night confusingly worse. And unwittingly, I found myself running in space like an astronaut, and seconds after (it seemed a fleeting eternity), I was hitting the solid reality that I had fallen into a deep ditch, headlong and a half (I nearly break my neck). To say the minimum, I was disoriented to the maximum.

While trying to gather what was left of my scattered wits and attempting to comprehend the night's events, I freaked out at where I was – in no-man's land (and alone). As I touched my Bible in my back pocket, asking God for a reprieve, I heard some movements close by, in the cane field. I didn't move a muscle and prayed in earnest. They jumped over the ditch and I heard the clutter of the helicopter's rotating blades and saw its searchlights as it traversed the field. Eventually, there was some form of quietness and I fell into an uncomfortable, tired and somehow deep sleep – in the ditch.

But before the cock could crow three times, I was on my feet and using the sound of vehicles on the highway, I found my bearings and was treading mystically – that is I had zero visibility profile all my way back to the city. When I showed up in the ghetto, I was greeted with the news that the other gang members had been rounded up and that the ring leader had been shot and wounded and was under armed guard at the hospital.

Well, though I have my (well-founded) fears about sea rides, I had to chance it before I was picked up in connection with the silly murder. And well, as you might realise, I am back on home turf.

Did you enjoy the ride? We were having so much fun – isn't it true?

THE
DRUG HUNTERS

Saturday afternoon came and my hunting buddy picked me up as he had promised at 4.00 pm. You see, the hunting season was open and we wanted variety when it came to our meat supplies. So we had decided to hunt some wildlife – in particular, agouti. (Incidentally, it was also the drug eradication season when the US army and local police would search our forest for marijuana plantations.) I had my newly acquired and licensed .22 rifle, and my partner, who is more experienced in staking out wildlife, had a 12-gauge shot gun and a haversack. And naturally, we also had our hunting permits.

So we drove up to one of the popular hunting grounds in the interior. As we got out of the vehicle my buddy (a baldhead) said slyly, "Rasta might throw one stone and kill two birds..." I wondered what he meant and was tempted to ask but it somehow slipped my mind.

I have a lot of reservations when it comes to trespassing on private property and voiced my feelings to my colleague. He told me that it was OK and he was accustomed to the region. He also mentioned that at that time most farmers are out of their fields and this was also the time when the wildlife come out to feed.

We had on full camouflage army fatigues like real US soldiers – to make it more difficult for the game to see us. (My outfit was donated by a cousin who served in the US army once upon a time; I don't know how my friend had acquired his.)

You know, I have a little difficulty in understanding the rationale behind our outlawing of camouflage outfits. I mean if I am thinking of making a coup, a camouflage suit is not a requisite. What I would need is an M16 or AK47, rocket launcher and so on. Do you understand?

So after patrolling for some time in the "heights", my partner suddenly motioned to me to be quiet and then I heard some noise in the undergrowth. It sounded like somebody doing an activity but the "expert" whispered that it was, in fact, an agouti. We cruised up on the source of the activity like commandos and came in sight of the game. It was unaware of our presence being engaged in eating a fallen banana bunch (agoutis love itals!) My partner offered me the option of making the first kill. I declined, oui! I didn't want to blow it. So my friend lined up his gun sights and fired. Blam! The sound was deafening and echoed in the surrounding hills. And although I was expecting it, it still frighten me.

Of course he was right on target. Bagging his kill in his haversack, we continued our search for more game and stumbled upon a track that didn't appear to be used much. My friend seemed keen to follow it so I tagged along close behind,

On approaching what looked like a clearing, the hunter advised me to tread carefully and avoid stepping on dry twigs to minimise detection by our prey. At a certain spot he made a sign to be still. I listened intensely but didn't hear anything like on the previous occasion. What I could hear, however, was voices. I wondered what was up. The area was cut off from civilisation. So we crept up on the source of the talking to make a reconnaissance.

What I saw made me shudder. It was one big cultivation of marijuana – maybe an acre or more. I whispered to my buddy: "Let us get the hell out of here."

"No," he said, "Let us wait awhile."

I reasoned, any way I watched it, it was dangerous. The cultivators were very likely to have fire power. Next worst-case scenario was if the drug hunters found us in the proximity of the plantation. We could be arrested as ganja cultivators (and that is plenty jail!)

I couldn't keep still (I was both anxious and restless). And unknowingly, I stepped back on a dry branch that snapped with a loud sound under my weight. The sound alerted the planters, and one with sharp eyesight, making out our camouflaged uniforms, shouted to the others: "Fellas! Police in the area!" There was a lot of commotion, and then I heard branches breaking violently under the bush. The planters were abandoning their camp and fleeing in all directions. They must have thought it was a full strength police patrol.

My hunting partner laughed. He was enjoying the idea of impersonating police officers. Entering the abandoned plantation, he started uprooting the cream of the crop: buds and tops (the sensemilla stalks). Their shack contained some of their equipment: bow saws, shovels, forks, watering cans, cutlasses, and other eating utensils, and some food supplies – they even had some food on a fire.

I noticed that their hut was built with ingenuity using inner tube to bind the posts and boards together. This was to avoid too much construction noise; they also had a green tarpaulin for the roof to conceal it from air surveillance.

You maybe thinking I was enjoying that scene too. No boy! You mad! I was afraid and longing to be back by our transport. If I had known the way back I would have left him. My partner, however, had other ideas. He commented, "Boy, good weed, oui! I can make a big money on that?" It was then I understood what he meant when he spoke of killing two birds with one stone. I told him, "That your mind tell you! A 'big jail' you will get instead."

But while we were in the middle of the ganja field and my partner was busy "fulling" his haversack, I heard the sound of a low-flying transport. I quickly ruled out the banana spray plane (I know the sound of the engine well) and identified the sound to be that of a flying chainsaw, a helicopter. I told my buddy, "That is the 'eradication' squad."

The helicopter came and hovered above the plantation with the down wind from its rotating blades causing havoc among the tall marijuana trees. We hit the dirt and crawled out of the area on our stomach like snakes amid the swaying ganja trees (it was a good thing we had on these woodland camouflage outfits). While creeping, I hoped that the soldiers would not use agent orange on us or firebomb the plantation.

As we reached the plantation's perimeter windbreak, I glanced back and saw "soldiers" baling out of the helicopter which was a couple of feet off the ground. We were not out of the woods yet because one spotted us and shouted, "Stop or I will shoot!" But it couldn't be me he was talking to because it was my turn to tear down the forest. I didn't wait for my friend to lead the way. I heard a burst of machine-gun fire and I just knew that it was down I was running, no matter what. I cleared all obstacles, getting a number of scratches and bruises in the process, and reached a stream I could remember us crossing earlier. I paused a while to catch my breath and check my bearings. On hearing some footsteps coming, I concealed myself in a bush. It was my friend, and yes oui! he was still carrying his haversack of cannabis.

The drug hunters did not hunt us down. They were maybe preoccupied with eradicating the God-made weed. So we made our way to our transport. It was getting very dark by then. I told my hunting friend "straight" that I was not going down Roseau with him if he insisted on carrying his illegal goods. (It had a strong perfumed type of smell: a sency odour that virtually makes it impossible to get it concealed.) So he agreed, and hid it in a bush saying he would return for it later. That gave me peace of mind and since that time I have not gone hunting again (positive).

So what I do with my gun? I hang it up nuh! (Turned it over to the cops for safe-keeping.) What else?

HANDS UP!

It wasn't too long ago that this happened to me. I was walking late at night down this almost deserted street in Roseau. You see, I had just come from watching an exciting North American basketball game on TV at a friend's home. (Do you know, we know more about what on in the NBA league than in our local league?) I was approaching a step opposite a lamp post that did its own thing – switched on and off at leisure (whenever it felt like) – when I noticed two men sitting there, conversing or whatever (or, maybe, planning!)

As I drew closer, the lamp on the utility pole suddenly went out. The street in question is not really a "bad" street, it is just that certain characters from near and far would come and hang out around. Then I saw that there was just one man was on the step; the other had disappeared. When I was adjacent to the step, the remaining guy suddenly got up and confronted me brandishing what looked like a sawn-off shot gun. It was! It must have been (maybe) a leftover from the dread era of the seventies when we had some gun-toting dreads in the hills.

The lone gunman uttered these unfamiliar words, "Hands up!" Playing innocent, I demanded for what?

"Just give me all the money you have on you", he replied in a business-like manner.

There was a light on in a nearby upstairs building so I raised my voice – hoping to attract attention – and said, "Boy, I doh have money on me! What you trying nuh man?"

"Doh give me that bullshit!" the outlaw responded,

Then, to my total dismay, the light upstairs went silent (it out). To me, it was saying in its own silent language "that is none of my business". I thought they might call the police, and say, "Look, an armed robbery in progress". Maybe they did and the cops didn't risk showing up. But should the next day reveal my corpse in the street, I knew people would say I heard this and that.

Anyway, I didn't like staring down the barrel of a sawn-off shot gun one bit. You maybe saying why I doh try a karate stunt? That does only work for heroes in movies. So I told the bandolero, "Take that out in my face before it go off accidentally." But he just ordered instead, "Turn out your pockets!"

I was going through the motions when, to my welcome relief, the light on the pole suddenly switched on again. The robber turned to the light on the nearby post and said, "I shooting you oui! Like a cowboy." And like as if it heard the threat, the lamp post out again.

I decided then to see if reason would prevail and took my time going through my pockets.

"So if you doh get money on me," I told him, "You going and shoot me then?"

"Maybe, I doh know yet" was his dubious response.

I made a wise crack. "What you want the money for, to go and parro and make yourself more stupid than you is already?"

"Shut up!" he snapped, and gave me a silly look (like as if anything could happen) and threatened me, "I... I shooting you oui." And my concerns were raised a couple bars because you should know that a fool with the upper hand is a dangerous combination. So I changed my programme and style and said, "If I had the money I would gladly give it to you because it is better to give than to receive."

"What kind of puzzle that?" he asked in a bewildered manner. I think he meant parable. At this point, the street light lit up again as the partner's partner made an appearance on the scene, seemingly out of nowhere, and put on a great Grammy award-winning act.

"What happening there?" he asked like an angel. I jumped the gun (took in front) and answered, "Your partner that want to hi-jack me there." It seemed he knew me from somewhere because he turned to his friend and asked, "But why you doing mister that for? You doh seeing mister haven't got money?"

"He have!" the gunman replied unconvinced.

"But look, I turned out all my pockets and I doh have nothing," I said.

"You lying! It in your shoes," the gunslinger replied.

My heart jumped because he was right. But I responded "You too stupid! My toes does smell so much. But the next time I passing there, I'll give all you some money. All you doh even bound to ask, just let me go home in one piece."

"Eh heh! Is me that more stupid you see. You will just go and call the police for us," the outlaw responded.

"No man," I countered, "I will never do that, who you take me for nuh?"

And his partner in crime said, "I know you," And he stated my name and surname in full.

I was taken aback. How come they know me so good, and I

didn't know them at all? "You know me so good," I said, "so I will always set all you up, what is your name so I can ask for all you..."

The partner in crime said, "I wouldn't tell you my real name, but people does call me Batman..."

"Oh, I see, if you is Batman then he must be Robbing Hood," I interrupted, looking at his partner. What I really wanted was the menacing gun pointing out of my direction. "Well, tell your partner," I continued, "to point the gun somewhere else nuh."

"But it empty, it haven't got bullets," revealed Batman.

"I always hear is empty guns that does kill people," I said, and used that seemingly amicable turn of conversation to take my hand and gently push the gunman's hand aside. As I did so, there was a flash of light and one loud explosion. Boom! The scatter shot shaved me! I felt the wind of it. I frighten! They frighten! The whole neighbourhood frighten! And the darkness started to light up as sleepers got this rude awakening.

The robbers dropped the gun and ran into the night in fright. I picked it up. It was luke-warm. Oooh, so empty guns can really kill people – I was now convinced. But before anybody could ask questions, which I doh like to answer, because it usually leaves you with too many additional questions to answer, I went on my business.

Well, no! I did not hand the gun over to the cops (if they were paying for it maybe I would). What I did was to dismount it, clean it, varnish it, and polish it and when I finish it (What? No, I didn't say, when I finish shit! Go over it again), kept it as a souvenir and a reminder of the night that Batman and Robbing Hood told me, "Hands up". Ha!

THE
BODYGUARD

In keeping with my line of work, as private investigator and sometimes security for hire, a youngster, who had a lot of faith in my prowess, even more than I had in myself, told me that he required my services urgently: "I want you to be my bodyguard tonight – and I'll be your pal," he said.

I guess you want to know what it is all about. Well what happened is a lot. So we will just browse through it quietly OK? Well, the boy extra troublesome, you know. And through unfortunate and, perhaps, complicated, circumstances he got involved in drugs. And presently, the boy had invested a grand in some "grams" (You doh know what is grams? Grams is powder. What kind of powder? You mean you that "off"? If that is the case…well I sorry for you.)

Anyway, the deal turned sour. Let me try to explain. The dealer kept reneging and reneging and failing to deliver – claiming "police hot" and so on and, "They shooting man…" A lot of "mamaguy", that's bullshit in street talk. So my unofficial client wanted me to accompany him into this "drug hole" in an effort to retrieve his investment. He seemed convinced that if I should just show up as his bodyguard, he would be reimbursed right away. His exact words were: "My boy, if you come with me – he paying me one time!"

You see, I have this deadly scar on my face. I'll tell you about it some other time. But first things first, before you accuse me of condoning bad vibes. I asked the boy: "Boy! Why you get involved in that for, eh?" He said that he wanted to make a quick money to buy a bike (so that he could impress – I guess). But he did not want his parents to know about his illegal activities and now, look complications, the "dealer" had his money in fire, therefore he wanted me to try something – anything – like a bad boy act, nuh.

Well I said I would give it a try, but reiterated that he was wrong! Dead wrong. I gave him a fatherly talk, saying, "Be not envious of evildoers and their riches, my son, because sudden destruction is their fall and destiny," and other such edifying lyrics. Do you understand? I would want to think so.

So we went into this "drug hole". And I was certainly not playing the part of a timid coward – though inside I was. The body language of most of the personnel present at that location was saying,"Who is that Rambo?" But between you and me it was more like "Rumbo" – I had two straight rum before getting into my act. Reaching a galvanize gate, my client friend indicated that that was the drug man's residence, I knocked the gate with authority (three times boldly) and heard the quick query, "Who's that?"

"Come and see!" I replied, in a positive attitude.

The dealer came to his gate, satisfied himself that it wasn't the drug squad, and opened up. And as soon as he saw the youngster behind me he knew what that visit was all about.

"I am here on my friend's behalf," I confirmed. "He told me that you and him have a deal – and that deal is not coming through – so he wants his money back, just like that!" I told him that I was the one that had laundered the money to the boy etc, etc. While talking I could see he was trying to recognise me, but I did not think he knew me – and even if he did he couldn't be sure. Contrary to expectation, there were no hostilities or hesitation from his quarter. He just said, "But, so long I tell the boy to come and get his money."

The youngster whispered, "He lying."

The drug man was on top of the scene, and continued, "I doh see why he had to bring you – like a bouncer for? I going for your money for you, but" – and the following was directed at the youngster, "You mustn't bring strangers by me."

He went indoors for the finance and I could see that two other persons were in his yard, two crack heads, who perhaps were checking their scene, blowing their brains out. But that wasn't my business.

The dealer returned and paid me for my client friend. I counted the dollars to verify, pocketed them and said to the dealer, "Ya – we safe! Take it easy…" and turned and left. But I still felt uneasy because we were in the drug hole and there was the possibility of an encounter with the cops who usually seek to pocket questionable funds when found on suspicious persons. So I was longing to exit this hole, and the sooner the better.

As we reached the end of a short cut, after a lamp post, two masked men jumped us. Armed with a knife, they demanded, "Give us all the money you have on you!" I was petrified (aka frightened) and told the robbers and myself simultaneously, "Take it easy – doh do nothing stupid." I realised it was a set up – and suspected the two characters in the drug man's yard, but what transpired after nobody could expect – not even you.

You may know that fear and desperation can sometimes do wonders – if not miracles. You see, there was a real possibility that I could make the newspaper headlines – I could just imagine them, "Man stabbed in drug hole – drug links suspected" and so on. Well, that last concern spurred me into desperate action. Suddenly, I exploded with a vicious kick to disarm the knifeman. The knife – fly from his hands – nobody doh see where it go! Before he could recover – in fear – I gave him one jump kick in his chest (I didn't want my kick to be under-powered – thus it was overpowered). He crashed backward into a galvanize fence and rebounded to an elbow in his jawbone. He hit the turf like a "close line".

His companion, startled by my blitz actions, realised too late that he should have fled already. He turned to flee, and I helped him on his way with a jump kick in his back like Bruce Lee – that powered him to a crash landing at the base of a rubbish bin. When I glanced back to the knifeman, I saw him making a desperate run for it. His accomplice likewise made a squealing escape like a rat. They had realised – belatedly – I was more of a true Rambo than a Rumbo.

My client looked bewildered. "Boy! I owing you!" he said. "If you wasn't there what would happen to me?" For sure he would have been robbed. Once you playing with fire, I told him, expect to get burnt – one way or the other.

But you can call me Rambo from now on and I'll be your bodyguard or comforter for life. You, dear reader, I talking to, oui!

CLOSE CALL

Where we going for this one? I am giving you the option of choosing this episode's location. You doh know? Oh boy, poor you! No imagination! So, I'll choose it. We going LA – Little Antigua, this time around. And I didn't "bang water" to reach there, I flew in.

So what I went and do there? It's OK. I'll tell you. For one, I wasn't in search of adventure, nor a story or episode material or whatever to share with you.

It was just an acquaintance from my past, who was (now) doing (extra) well in LA. I do not want to go into his alleged line of work – but will say in an allusion – it's the same story everywhere (Do you follow world affairs?) But my acquaintance was extra excited – he had fathered a kid over there. So ecstatic was he that he called me over on my cell to give me the good news and invite me over to celebrate its christening.

If you're a true fanatical fan of mine you might be aware that I have had a number – if not a record – number of close calls and brushes, both with King Death and also with various laws in DA, Guada, etc, which, especially the latter, has caused me to become (so to speak) a notorious local literature hero – and thus – "larger than life". Am I bragging? Can't you see the evidence? But this one is truly something else.

It was a Sunday morning; the christening party took place in a shantytown of notorious repute. And it was to be, by all indications, a marathon session. All types of illicit and legal substances to be abused were available, and in abundant supply – just name it. Yes oui! All that too. But how did you know? And there was enough music too – plus eats, plenty.

But I do not partake in the other abuses. Alcohol? Yes, a little. But certainly not those on the "black" list. Thus naturally, I could not be, nor feel at home in this ghetto yard though I was encouraged to do so by the host, who had paid all my expenses. But I did not find the environment to be to my liking so it was difficult to let my hair down.

I felt a premonition that a police drug bust was imminent. So being a person who tends to take only calculated risks – although, I'll admit, sometimes my calculations go haywire, I first sought to identify a possible escape route should my fears materialise. And I saw one. It was a bit difficult, but possible. Because of the sloping hillside nature of the ghettohood, it would have to be a rooftop getaway; the houses were of a step-like formation, going down to the street some distance away.

So the party was in full swing, going down about midday. And my friend was disturbing the neighbourhood. And one particular neighbour, I heard her complaining about the marathon session of noise, music and what-have-you. "Me going to call the police!" she said in my hearing. So I related that statement to my friend but he downplayed that scene telling me he was accustomed to that busybody

And after being served (drinks) a number of times, I was on the verge of becoming complacent too – in this foreign region. And, like in a dream, I suddenly heard a battering down on the yard fence. And one concerned individual shouted: "Police raid!" but no one had to tell me, I knew that already, oui!

Putting my contingency plan into action, in the twinkling of an eye I had climbed the galvanize fence and like a fiddler on the roof was leaping from roof to rooftop. My friends, I certainly did not go to Antigua to taste their jail (innocently). But when I landed on a rooftop like a burst of a thunder clap, I heard someone in the house, shriek: "O me Gad!" And on the next roof, I heard: "Wee, bon Dieu. Soucou!" In that split second my reasoning told me, indeed, a Dominican living in that one.

But there is a sage saying: "Look before you leap!" That is indeed commendable because while I was in mid-air, and about to land on the roof before the last, by the roadside, I observed that the galvanize was corroded, and realised instantly that it was the remains of a burnt-out shack. I wanted to abort the landing but that was irreversible, thus I crashed into it like a human missile.

And there was a solar eclipse, I thought. As the sunlight got blotted out by a rising column of thick, black charcoal dust and ashes. For quite a while I was in a dazed state, trying to comprehend the happenings – I had no useful knowledge. I did not know whether I was alive or dead.

The dust settled, and I emerged from my crash site still starry-eyed like a zombie, and saw approaching me two officers of the Royal Antiguan police regiment. I conceded arrest, thinking it futile to try and evade the law after that near disaster. But then the strangest thing happened. The officers asked if I had seen a fugitive fleeing. My boy, I was so dumbfounded that I was speechless. They must have thought that I was deaf, mute and dumb because they turned and went on their way and their wild goose chase. I was further disoriented.

After the cops had gone, the neighbours gathered around to see who was that stuntman. Perchance I glanced into a car's side window and could not recognise my reflection. And so I took a closer look in the side mirror and saw that I black like a tar baby! I sure wasn't looking black and beautiful. My two white eyes and teeth stood out against my black facial background and the colour of my outfit had mutated – it's no wonder the cops did not recognise me..

Well, the cops found some scraps of this and that and so on at my friend's home. I offered my condolences for his unfortunate incident, but he reassured me: "Doh hurt your head – my boy – I safe!"

I guess, it is the same sh…er, corruption story everywhere.

CONFESSIONS

Taking a break from my busy schedule a couple months ago, I was walking around town for a breather when I came across this old acquaintance. He was a far cry from the person that I once knew. He was a person who had it all but didn't appear to have it all again.

After giving me a fist tag street greeting, he asked me to loan him a "tenfer". But before endorsing the loan, I had to ask him, "Boy, what really happen to you? You wasn't so before."

He shook his head, and said, "Man I parro out!" His honesty made an instant impression. Addicts don't usually accept that they do have a problem. Realising the possibility of a good story, I told him, "Let us go and drink a beer and tell me all about it." (So that I could write all about it and you could then read all about it.) So we went to the closest bar —people seeing me in the company of this character maybe said, "Mister parro too!"

"But tell me something, what happen to your job?" I asked as we sat there drinking our beers.

"So long I lose that," he replied.

"How come you lose it?"

"I doh really, really lose it you know, I know where it is, but somebody else have it."

I continued my line of inquiries, "So why they fire you?"

"The bossman say I was touching his things," he said, sipping his beer.

"What happened to the transport you had?"

"I parro that man," he replied. What he meant was that he had sold it in whole or in parts for cocaine.

"So what about the place you was renting?"

"So long they kick me out," he said bluntly.

"And what about your personal effects?"

"I doh tell you, I parro everything already, the video, TV, tape, fridge, table, chairs, bed—I sell all that and cheap!" he admitted dolefully..

I interrogated him further. "So what about your girl, doh tell me you parro her too?"

"No man," he confessed, "She that parro me! She fired me and moved in with another guy."

Thinking aloud, I said, "Boy, is a good thing I didn't venture down that drug street." When he heard that, he said, like a Yankee, "I have been in some deep shit, men," and proceeded to give me his drugs story.

"Men, I started off like nearly every other parro head, smoking my little spliffs. I was in my teens then and had no drug problems because I didn't have to steal, beg or borrow to satisfy any cravings. The only problem was the occasional searches by the cops. Anti-ganja propagandists used to say then that weed was bad to our health and well-being, but when we experimented with that stuff the negative side effects propagated did not materialise, to our minds. That is just why the present warning about the dangers of harder substances do not register in youths' minds until it is way too late.".

Being curious, I asked, "But how did you fall into rock in the first place?"

"Well," he said, "it was simple. I got curious and tried it once with the pursuance of so-called friends, and that was it, marriage at first taste! Damn, I was stuck on it like crazy glue." He continued, "Men, I am so sick…whenever I see a piece of silver foil paper, I am tormented – it acts like a stimulant to me and I have to stop and pick it up to see what is in it."

"But why?" I asked.

"That is what they use to wrap these pieces of crack, men."

"So, what are the effects like?"

"When you smoke that," he replied, "you get big ideas; things materialise that are non-existent and you start to hallucinate and see gremlins and you feel guilty and get suspicious for nothing. Man, that does just screw up the way you think, believe me."

(I did.) I then asked, "How can I recognise a big dealer?"

"Some of them guys are undercover," he answered. "They launder their money, in buses, houses, land and other business, and drive around in big cars, men, with big engines."

"So you mean everybody that have V6s and V8s and 'night riders' in that then?"

"Not really," he said. "Some are genuine but… when you see some of them, raise your eyebrows."

"So you have no plans of quitting?" was my last question. And he declared, "Man, every day I pray to Jehovah to let me turn my life around."

The liquid in the beer bottles had run out by then. I dug into my pocket and pulled out a $100 bill, my last one, and presented it to him. He appreciated that to the max. He thanked me with a knuckle tag and left and I, too, went my way.

That happened some months ago so let us fast forward to recently. Just the other day I ran into the same dude and I can tell you it was a totally different story. He was a far cry from the guy I had spoken to a couple of months ago. The man was neat, looking irie, big, fat, etc. I had to ask again, "What happen? You are a Christian or what, or was in the jail?" (The "rest', as we call it.) They usually come out looking so, ie, better than those on the outside.

"No man, I rehabilitate!" he told me with a big smile. "Come let us go and drink some beers and I will tell you all about it, so you can spread the word."

He knew about my undercover writing and this time he bought the beers. He said to me, "You see, the 'black' note you gave me some months ago." I nodded, and he continued, "Well, I took it and bought some pieces of rock and blew my brains out. I was so spaced out in my old shack, I couldn't move. All I could do was just stare at the celotex in the ceiling and count the designed ventilation holes in it, about two million, over and over. When the effects of the high were over, I asked myself: 'Is so they put me nuh?' I realise that there was so much better use that I could have put that money to, and I just said, 'That's it! No more rock for me!'"

"Just like that?" I asked.

"No man," he replied. "It was coupled with the thought that while I was hustling for money to put in the drug man's pocket, he would pass me by in his dark-glass mafia car and laugh at me. I could feel it."

Knowing how tough it is to get off drugs, I asked, "How did you really do it?"

"It is not an easy road," he beamed. "But if you have the will you can do it, and if you ask the Most High, he will help. What I did was to retreat to the countryside far from any source of drug activities and chilled for six months, and I got the best high, a natural one. It was so good to know that I could fight the power and overcome it. And when I returned to the city I never frequented the drug places and friends who use that stuff and if ever I should get the urge, I drink some cold water instead because the drug high doesn't last long anyway."

I marvelled and questioned, "So you have managed to kick the habit for good?"

"I don't know," he replied, "the struggle continues and it is not really over till you are six feet under. It is easy to relapse but for the time being I feel good."

"I like the both sides of your story," I confessed to him, "and I am going to write about it. What is your advice to youths who might read it?"

He said somberly, "I'll tell them to stay far from crack and do not touch it. You'll regret it. You might not be lucky like me because drugs is a dead-end street."

We had another beer, and parted company. And really, I can't add anything much to what he said, but "crack kills" both physically and spiritually. That's it!

RETURN OF DAVID

We were in a popular bar drinking our weekend waters when one of my colleagues mentioned a "David". That name triggered a chain reaction and my thoughts started to reverse down memory lane, and my last encounter with a "David" became vivid like it was yesterday.

There had been this "David" with a notorious reputation. The first thing we had heard about him was that he had killed a man twice his size while still a teenager. So, when the news broke that David was coming to our town, we did not know how to cope. We were unprepared. Some thought he was bluffing and that he would not have the audacity to show his face. Little did we know that he would really come. Some even thought that if he dared to come we would make a pre-emptive strike and stop him dead in his tracks. We trusted in our mountains – our first line of defence.

That mystic day opened with no hint as to what was to happen later down. The first sign that this David was really coming to town occurred in the morning when I saw the seagulls that would normally be flying out at sea, virtually walking up inland for shelter. (The winds were getting too difficult to fly against.) Oh ho, you know now which David I referring to!

We thought we could handle David. His radical cousin, Hurricane Jannette, had passed so long ago that we couldn't remember what she did. So we were complacent. That is why a couple of friends and I (we were young and careless at the time) went driving around the city poking fun at those who took the threat seriously. We had no idea what was to come.

As the intensity of the winds grew, we were (at least I was) aware that the streets were becoming deserted. I noticed that a sudden gust of wind made a barricade lie down flat in seconds, but we still didn't take that sign seriously.

We were driving up the suburb of Goodwill (I was at the controls) when our mini-bus ran into difficulties against the head winds. I went into low gear but to no avail. The bus stalled on the brow of Federation Drive. Not only that, you know, it actually started pushing the bus back down the hill. All the time I am applying the footbrake and pulling the handbrake like mad. The wind reversed the bus into a utility pole.

So we were there, held up in the bus, wondering what's next? One of my friends exclaimed, "Look!!", and pointed up Goodwill. I know – you cannot imagine what I saw: but it was like the whole of Goodwill was coming down: galvanize, roofs (in whole and in parts), trees, branches, bicycles, fridges, washing-machines, a Volkswagen – all kinds of objects, just name it, they were coming. You know you could actually see the wind because of the luggage it was carrying.

When the barrage hit the bus I thought we were in a war zone. And we had to duck extra low in the bus for cover. The windshield got shattered and all types of missiles entered the bus. And some left without a trace. We now realised it was a serious thing and started praying feverishly.

We fled from the bus and took shelter on the west side of a two-storey building because the wind was bearing down from the east. It started whistling at an extremely high pitch so high that I feared for my hearing. And suddenly we were aware that there was light in the building. It now had a sun roof. The galvanize roof was gone and all the furniture and other appliances downstairs ascended and were ejected by way of the open roof because of the vacuum created when the roof took leave.

So we made a desperate dash amidst the flying debris and galvanise, which were like flying guillotines, to an old garage that was like a bomb shelter being well protected with walls about two feet thick, and its roof was a concrete decking. There we met other refugees and, although it had no doors or gate, it served its purpose.

You know, the wind had so much speed and rain that we could not see the other side of the street (which was just about 15ft away), when it was in its "full glory" (speeds well in excess of 150mph). Suddenly, without warning a UFO entered the bunker like a bullet! We just heard the sound of it ricocheting off the walls. Up to this day I have no idea what it could have been but luckily no one was hit or hurt.

When the first half was over, we emerged from hiding shell shocked. We were walking in a daze, like zombies. It was like a nuclear bomb had fallen: galvanize was twisted and littered the barren landscape; Goodwill resembled a big rubbish dump. There were few trees left on the mountains and those still standing had no leaves. (For months after there was no shaded vegetation.) The devastation was unbelievable. The naturalist dreads in the hills must have had an awesome display of the forces of nature.

My first "normal" thought came on my mother. Was she

OK? Did the old shack survive? We thought it was strong enough but now I wondered if it still existed. I made my way through the debris of fallen trees, branches and utitility poles to my home. It was still standing. It was a strong son of a house! It had been built by carpenters of old who used wooden pins instead of nails to hold the main structure together. But the galvanize had gone. I brought her to a neighbour who had a "fortress" and offered her shelter.

Then I went sightseeing with my friends. When we entered Roseau, it was mass confusion, but this is an understatement. But every Tom, Dick and Harry plus Ann and Mary were doing their shopping, ie looting. And strange enough money wasn't on their minds – it had no value, there was nothing to spend it on. Because, for the next six months, the population depended on US and British army combat rations, and secondhand clothes and supplies donated from countries that pitied us. We, the population, were now on one level – equally destitute. So there it was, we were helping ourselves to eats and drinks. Imagine, my friends and I downed a bottle of whisky without any chaser, and we never felt a hint of a high (we were so cold and wet).

And without a hint, the second half started, and Hurricane David commenced shooting in the opposite direction and we were caught napping once again. We made a mad scramble for cover carrying a carton of alcohol. Most of what trees and houses that were spared in the first half of play were finished off. David just completed his mission of total destruction – 95%.

When the all clear sign was given, we all went shopping

again. Business houses that somehow survived the onslaught of David felt the wrath of our hammers and ripping irons. There were gigantic give aways by all the leading business places downtown, and at the harbour everybody was clearing goods out of customs at random.

My boy, I have some fond memories of David, but today, whenever some hear about hurricane "they fraid", while others are getting their hammers and ripping irons ready. David, I can not forget you. Trust me.

LOST AT SEA

I have this friend, who has a fishing boat, a 20 footer, and he usually brings me fresh fish to make my Sunday fish broth. He had said to me, "You like fish so much, why you doh take a trip with me one of these Sundays?"

Though I like fish, I don't like being sea-borne. I have this memory of my vagabond days when we took a big tube and went bathing in the sea, and either the wind or sea currents took us out to sea. We struggled to paddle back to shore but it was of no use, so we had to abandon tube and swim to shore.

Now, it seemed he was holding a gun to my head, so reluctantly I agreed to take the trip the coming Sunday. But ... I told my fishing friend that we should get some safety gear – life jackets, flares, a compass, mirror, two-way radio and food supplies.

"We doh need that man," he commented. "We doh going far, just there we going, oui."

"Just there we going!?!" I echoed in a different tone.

"What you worrying about?" he went on. "My engine working good!"

"Your engine working good??" I repeated uncertainly.

"But I wouldn't risk my life," he declared. "If anything happen we in the same boat."

"If anything stupid happen, before I die I killing you with my bare hands," I assured him. He laughed because he considered me a weakling.

When Sunday morning came, I went to church and after

service bought some personal supplies: fresh bread and a tin of corned beef. I put on some home clothes and went down to the boat house. The fisher of fishes was there, his boat already on the sea.

"Boy so long I waiting for you," he shouted. "I even say you not coming again."

"I come out and say my prayers," I stated. "I doh know if I will get a watery grave."

"You is a big joke boy, just outside Possy we going."

"What! right Portsmouth!?!" I exclaimed. "You have enough gas nuh? It is best we buy more gas boy." He told me that he had enough gas to reach Guadeloupe and to come back. I hopped on board and out we went to a spot outside Portsmouth that he stated was a good fishing zone. We travelled parallel to the coast line – I was watching the distance and thinking if anything abnormal happened I could, at least, swim to shore.

We went a good way beyond Portsmouth, but we could still see Morne Diablotin, Dominica's highest mountain. The weather was irie, clear and fair and we took out our fishing rods and bait and started fishing. My friend was right, there was fish in abundance, and I soon mastered the techniques and art of deep-sea fishing.

The first clue that the weather had changed was when it started raining. "Best we go back oui, we have enough fish," I suggested. He agreed, saying that land was "in this direction". No, I countered, it is in that direction. By this time the sea was misty white. He won, of course – it was his boat – so we started up and made for what he thought was land. I had my fingers crossed. After travelling into the unknown for some time, I told him, "If you was right we shoulda jam Dominica already!" He turned about, but for all I knew we could have been going round in circles. After a seemingly endless time, he said, "We lose oui."

"I know that, I had warn you!" I replied.

"So you want to kill me now?"

"No! Not yet, but we shoulda bring a compass!" I reminded him.

"So what we can do now?" he asked dejectedly.

"Nothing nuh," I replied. "Switch off the engine. We might need the gas to reach land or help when the weather clear up." He followed my advice.

We were now at the mercy of the open sea. When I took a look at my watch it was 4.40pm. I realised that we would be spending the night on the waters unless a miracle happened.

We ate some of my recess but it wasn't as tasty as it should have been and I knew we had to stretch it as far as possible. I wondered how long it would take before the local coast-guard would be notified. This was one time I would have welcomed their presence. I also knew the chance of finding us on this wide and open sea was very faint.

I prayed and prayed again. I hoped that in the night the weather would clear up and we would see some beckoning lights, or that the next day we would see land – any island would be excellent. But that was wishful thinking because for the next five days (I would have lost track of the days if not for my watch data) there was no sign of life, no floating branches, not even seagulls. All we saw was the sun rising out of the sea and setting into the sea again. The bread and corned beef lasted three days. What we survived on after? Sun-dried and sun-baked fish. It took guts and no glory to eat it. We put some sea water on the fish (for to get it as tasty as possible). I swore that if I survived that I would never dispute the price of fish with any (true) fisherman again. We saw some planes flying so high above they looked very small to us, and I imagine we must have been invisible to them in this deep blue sea.

On the seventh day, we saw a boat. It wasn't big but it lifted our spirits. We rowed to it but the two guys on board were worse off than we were. They were St Lucians and had been drifting for two weeks (at least that is what they said). We tied our boats together, but they were so hungry that they ate the rest of our fish. I wondered if after two weeks I would still be alive!

I couldn't understand how anyone could willingly go on a hunger strike. I felt weak and sick, my inside was eating away at itself. I was certain that I would not see Dominica again, neither my girl nor my mother, my Old Queen. I knew she would take it bad. She had warned me not to go and I myself didn't want to go either (when your mind or intuition tells you something, you shouldn't doubt it).

On the 15th day, just before sunset, I thought I could make out land. There were little lights twinkling on the horizon. "Look! Land ahoy!" I shouted like Christopher Columbus. I was excited, my heart raced. I tried to get my companions' attention but they were so weak, they just mumbled like they were delirious. I shook the tank of gasoline. It sounded half-full. So I prayed to my creator and saviour and cranked the engine, and, at the third go, it burst into life. I made a beeline for land, but about two or three miles out, the engine ran out of fuel. "Let us row, that might be our only chance," I begged the guys. But my plea fell on deaf (if not dead) ears. So I put my back on the oar and struggled. Then suddenly, I was aware of the best music I have ever heard in my short life. The sound of a marine motor. My boy!!! It was the US coast-guard. Words certainly couldn't express my joy.

The next thing I can remember is waking up in a US Virgin Islands hospital, taking drips. The immigration official said we were lucky because we were about to drift into the rough and merciless Atlantic Ocean. They notified our families, who had given up on finding us alive. (They thought it was a drug deal that had gone sour. Trust them.)

My mother was delighted. "OK. Once you still alive, and I can see you in flesh and blood, I can die now," she said. But, you see the sea, I respect it to the "fullest", and fishermen, nuff respect to you. But you doh hearing? My girl already had another man, oui!

TIME WARP

This one is one of my creepier, weird and freaky adventures. Truly it's stranger than fiction, but was it really an adventure? Tell me what you think of it when you are through (reading).

It started when I and some acquaintances decided to have a "jam up", a "mess" (ie, a cook up) one weekend in Virgin Lane, in the proximity of a place called "Baghdad". The session lasted late into the night and along the way a number of bottles of Night Train wine became casualties and dominoes were being body slammed – all night – till the wee hours of the morning.

And well around one o'clock, when things were simmering down, I decided to go and sleep, by my second home – my girl's house up in Harlem (aka Newtown). But before saying my farewell to the crew in the vicinity – they cracked some stupid jokes about Jombie "Ba waying" (road blocking) me on my way because they know I had to go through the two cemeteries on Bath Road, en route to Newtown. But I was too high for that to trouble or concern me. I mean a devil like me?! Jombie 'fraid me! (that I would want to think).

Anyway, I left, and travelled the lonely Bath Road going to Newtown. But just as I reached the entrance of the Botanical Gardens' gate, and the section between the two burial grounds, there was a black out – they take lights! And that sobered me a bit. I felt a strange creepy, chilly feeling – like Jombie in the area. Thus I was, to be truthful, afraid to walk the gauntlet. So I hung out by the Gardens' gate, waiting and hoping to get a companion to walk through this – er – superstitious habitat of the dead.

And one turned up. His apparition was that of a phantom but that I condoned, overlooked, because I was glad! Boy! Very glad! It was an aged man. I asked him where he was heading and he stated, "Charlotteville", an ancient name for Newtown. I related to him my purpose for going to Newtown and he confessed that, in his heyday, he was just the same: had plenty woman (but there was no "help" in those days). Midway through the cemetery crossing I confided in him, "Boy, is a good thing I meet you to walk through the two cemeteries. Everybody tell me that it does have Jombie there."

He replied, "That they used to tell me too – when I was alive!" My boy! I get one shock! And experienced horripilation as my hairs stood up straight. I heard a fading, mocking, devilish laugh as he did a disappearing act. I did a right about turn – and you talk about run! Ben Johnson is a joke!

When I arrived back in Virgin Lane I was breathless –and panting like a dog. But strangely, after a little pause to catch my breath, and to regain my wits after my little walk with a walking dead, I found the setting of the place to be different – the houses looked unfamiliar. I asked an elderly couple, still awake and roasting coffee, about my friends who lived in the immediate area – and they answered that they had no knowledge of the persons I was referring to.

Oddly, I was talking in English but they were answering me in Creole (aka patois). I asked again, what time did they take electricity? And they were lost by the term "electricity", and my understanding became more mystified, more so when I made the astonishing discovery that there was a total absence of electricity wires and utility poles in the lane.

I went back into the night street disoriented. And noted there was a marked absence of motorised vehicles parked along the road, and I realised also that the streets were unpaved – just stone works reminiscent of slavery days. Well, I forgot about Newtown – and is home I want to go, but the question is, how, because I was now in a strange world and not of my making. I was unrealistically convinced that somehow I had experienced a "time warp", and had slipped from the brink of the 21st century and back into the 19th century.

So I descended, what I knew as Constitution Hill, and saw a number of push carts with big, spoked, iron wheels and barrels of whatever parked along the streets. And again – noticeably – there weren't any high-rise buildings. Reaching the Cork Street junction, I saw a big bright light approaching me from the Lagoon area – and straightway my imagination suggested that it was a soucouyant (a witch). Thus I started up Cork Street, in the direction of the police headquarters, for refuge. Glancing back, I saw that the big light had dimmed and I visualised a shadowy figure stalking me up the street. To my mind, it was the soucouyant – in person!

My boy, first time I feel scared so! My inside turned watery. When I came to the Acme Garage area, it was not there. The street was blocked by a wall and plenty bushy shrubs. My escape cut off, I turned to see that that "daughter of a witch" was almost on top of me. And she certainly wasn't pretty. First time I witnessed a creature, so black and ugly! My boy or girl! I was a bag of fear – trembling all over.

This wretched witch kept approaching closer and closer and I felt her cold-blooded hands attempting a stranglehold on my neck. And funny, the only person I thought could save me now was my dear mother. Thus I called out loudly and frantically "MAMIEEE…!" and felt one hot slap!

I frighteningly jumped up – I did not have time to contemplate offering my other cheek for another hot slap because suddenly lights came back! And it was now broad daylight, as I heard the DJ on the radio, also the CNN news flash on the war in Kosovo – and simultaneously – the telephone ringing; also, I heard vehicles in the streets, and a loud horn blast of a big truck trucking through the streets outside PRRAAMMPP!! I was suddenly back into the appropriate timing of time – 1999!

My girl chided me: "How dare you be sleeping big day like that!?!…" No! I didn't hit her back, I am not that kind of person, but it was almost a time warp, wasn't it! I guess you might conclude that it was just another weird dream.

THE
IMPOSTER!

By now, you ought to know me better, and you have probably realised I like to act and fantasise etc. But, quite unintentionally, I recently found myself impersonating a police officer. Look, so it happen ... I not lying nuh!?

One afternoon, I was watching my army suit (complete – cap to boots) – the same one I was wearing during my jungle adventure in The Drug Hunters. (Did you read that classic?) And I thought that after months of watching it "watch me" (it was well hung up in hanger etc), I would don it again later in the evening and make a patrol round the block downtown, and "pose up" with my peers.

But you may also be aware that there is a silly law outlawing that popular military outfit that I love so bad (for true!). You see, I had always wanted to be a commando – I can recall vividly shoplifting "commando" comic books back in my teens. (Sshh! Doh tell nobody.) But the stupid law works like this: if you're modelling a camouflaged shirt, or a cap, boots, scarf, or a short-pants version, a dress or skirt – it's no problem! But if it is a long pants! Boy, you mad! Is like, you have a coup on your mind – whether you are unarmed and un-dangerous. That is the law's obnoxious rationale. But where was I?

OK (I've got it), so night came, and I dress up in my camouflage suit, and proceeded to make my debut on the blocks in downtown. On my way I noticed a number of curious persons trying their utmost to recognise just who was that soldier? Who tell you? Me oui! The imposter! Walking like a Rambo, full of morale!

But as I approached a stop line and street corner and junction in Roseau, I synchronised, coincidentally, with a high-ranking police inspector in a car, accompanied by his wife and family. Well, I figure my mind was slow because I did not give him the "Heil Hitler" salute, which is customary to be performed by privates, in such circumstances or instances etc. It would appear he loved the attention he received from such protocol but, as you can deduce, I wasn't the wiser to such knowledge. He must have thought it lack of respect. Thus, he called on me, "What is your name, number and rank?"

I replied, "But Sir, I not a police, nuh." He retorted, "Then, young man, what are you doing in these military fatigues?" I stammered a bit saying "Sir, Sir, I, I didn't know it was illegal… (a big lie oui!) … I see everybody using it, and they selling it all about…"

"If you know what is good for you," he said with a voice of authority, "just remove these clothes right away!"

I retorted: "But Sir, if I take out all my clothes, people will say, I mad!"

"But you are!" he replied, and continued, "Go home and remove it right away before I call for assistance…" I wanted to argue my point of view but some sense prevailed. So I gave him his due respect saying, "OK Sir! Yes Sir! Right away, Sir! And thank you, Sir!"

He drove off and I went a little further up the street and turned into a short cut, to backtrack to home, on The Hill. Navigating between the unorthodox galvanize fencing, I stumbled on a drug deal (that I assume), and was rather perplexed and taken aback by the commotion and literally "chewing up" of the fences by two dealers in their desperation to get away: they thought I was a cop!

But one youngster, poor guy, froze in 100% fright. I guess it was a déjà vu scene for him. Instinctively, I held his hand, and it was cold to the touch, and I could hear his heartbeat pounding in his chest, "Doom! Doom!" etc like a bass drum, and suddenly sweat (cold sweat!) started flowing profusely down his brows. And, well, is now I started to hear stammering! 'C, c, c…Sir, please, please, my, my granny," – I doh know where "Granny" coming in – "that send me, me, me to buy that for her and and…" I realised he was going to tell me his whole life story. Therefore, I told him, "Relax, take a deep breath and talk to me." He attempted, swallowed, and nearly stifled. When I examined his hands, there was the evidence – a couple of joints, crushed up and soaking wet – from sweat.

"Boy, what for me to do with you, boy, eh?" I asked. He couldn't reply. His voice box was mute. "Let us go up!" I said, and he readily conceded arrest, like a sheep to the slaughter. And suddenly bright in my awareness was a piece of Bible study, where one was pardoned and his debt cancelled, and, he, in turn, turned around and victimised one who was indebted to him. So I played like I had a change of heart and said, "Boy, before your granny die on your account, go, and do the lady message for her eh," And I held the evidence, and crushed it under heel, like a cowboy, and made him pledge to "put up some resistance" and resist "crack cocaine" specifically, then released him.

The boy face changed (for the better) but he couldn't believe it or move. I told him, "If, I count to three, and you still there, I re-arresting you, and commenced, "One"… he backed away; "Two..." he turned about; and, before I could say, "Three..." he kicked dust and disappeared. I laughed (internally).

I doubled back to my shack, took off my army costume and put on my regulars: oversized jeans, American cultured T-shirt and Nikes and returned to street life.

But while descending The Hill, I re-encountered the same youtman under a lamppost, relating to his peers, his brush with the law. I heard him saying: "Boy! God that save me oui! All now so, I would be in the cell." When he saw me, he said, "The police looking just like mister." Feeling slightly guilty, I said, "It must have been my brother. But you lucky! He doesn't give people break! You better kneel down and pray boy!"

"I saying that too, oui!" he replied.

So what do you think? If I was a cop, would you consider me a good cop or a bad cop? Speak up! Louder! I can't hear you.

MY LAST SUPPER

I was introduced to this wealthy businessman, who said that I was a writer extraordinaire. You know I didn't know how to cope with the compliment and so blushed (100%). I would have felt much better had he given me a big slap or pat on the back and said, "Boy you is something else!" Imagine, I could not even say, "Thanks for the compliment" or something so. I just stood there stuttering without words, "Eh, eh, eh, eh."

I mean, we know people never give Jack his jacket while he is alive; they would rather down press him and tell him he is a jackass. But when he is gone forever to the city of peace, they then admit, "Jack was a jolly good fellow and we are missing him." Therefore, I was extremely flattered to be recognised by so great a person (a businessman oui!!!) while I was still alive.

He compounded my dilemma by inviting me to his mansion house for supper. He said that he wanted to tell his grand and great-grandchildren, that he had had supper with a "King Author". Boy, I was embarrassed to the max. But I couldn't duck it because I wanted him to help publish this book. He is the one who advised me to "make a short story of short stories". (I think he meant a medley of short stories.) Anyway, I felt a little safe because I was the only guest so no one could disseminate the bad news should I misbehave – like when I was invited to The Dinner (you read that one?). I felt also that I could put on a better performance this time around because I can be a great pretender when I am ready.

To tell the truth, I felt honoured to be invited to his home.

You should see me in his "air-con", power this, power that, fully loaded computerised car. He boasted that it cost him a hundred and plus grands. (That made me believe he was picking money on trees or was involved in the drug trade and was using that businessman approach as a smoke screen.) And, as you know, there are numerous allegations about the involvement of big business people and other top-ranking officials being in it. But anyway, I enjoyed that car ride, going down and up Belfast, our local Beverly Hills.

The guy had automatic gates and a state of the art garage, hi-tech automated door and lights. If I was a little more ignorant, I would have said, "He dealing with the devil!" But the first thing that caught my attention was his big alarm dog in a cage outside. It was reminiscent of the one that chased me during the effects of The Big Splash (Did you read that classic too?). He told me that he fed it on whole chicken legs, and imagine a big writer like me have to settle for chicken back and neck.

So he introduced me to his wife and family. The wife was pretty – very much so – and he also had a son (who is of little interest) and an extra beautiful ebony daughter, who literally put her mother in the shade. Hence I was forced to put on a splendid, gentleman-like performance; I didn't want to show off my true (dirty) colours.

After the meal, the son and daughter excused themselves and went upstairs to do their homework (or watch TV), and the wife went to the kitchen to do some cleaning up while he and I sat there discussing how to go about financing the publication of this most exciting and entertaining book.

I do not know how it happened but the front door was ajar, and the next thing I saw was his big dog poking its nose in and growling. So I said in 100% concern, "Look, your dog coming inside oui." I really thought that he had his dog under heavy manners, like he (apparently) had the rest of his household. But I realised that something was very, very wrong when he exclaimed in full-fledged fright, "My dog?" For a guy pushing 50, he was fast and agile; for in a flash, he was on the table and diving through the closest window.

His actions caught me napping. I had to assess my situation in record-quick time. It was much too late to run. My only defensive move was to go on the offensive and so I attacked the dog, engaging it in mid-air as it leapt for my forearm which I forced into its throat. But I knew that my meg (thin) arms would be chicken feed for a dog of its stature. So I sank my teeth into its neck. I thought, bite for bite, let us see who biting harder. Man, that was a serious dog fight, taking place between the drawing room and the dining room.

When the wife heard the commotion, she quickly realised what was happening and came to the dog's rescue. It appears that she was the only one who could approach the dog – I guess because she feeds it. She had to literally get me off the dog with a broom saying, "Mash! Mash! Leave the dog alone." When I finally did, it squimmered and squealed and retreated with its tail between its legs whimpering as it went. It realised that I was a much bigger dog than it thought it was.

Well, I was taken to hospital to have the injury to my forearm dressed. The dog's owner compensated me with a healthy sum of money, plus he was more than glad to be associated with the publication of this book.

So, you see, that experience also added another story to my compilation. And you maybe enjoyed it at my arm's expense, and, my boy, that was my last supper outside of my ranch. And, hear that, apart from the wife, I am the only other person who can approach that dog these days. Is like I am its best friend, oui!